CW00881918

First published by Amazon Kindle in January 2013

This edition – second edition, 2014

The Man in the Corner © Hayden Gribble 2013

All rights reserved

Cover design © John Galantini 2014

ISBN-13: 978-1500549862

ISBN-10: 150054986X

THE MAN IN THE CORNER

HAYDEN GRIBBLE

CHAPTERS

For Grandad

CHAPTER ONE

THE MAN IN THE CORNER

The man looked up from his cold breakfast at the clock above the counter. 10:08. He had been sitting in the corner of the restaurant for nearly 40 minutes. He pondered for a moment, pausing to gaze out into the harsh November street, cold and unwelcoming, mirroring perfectly the look in his eyes. They were puppy dog blue yet seemed as chilling as a bead of ice trickling down the spine. The man rarely had time to stop and think about his job and what he was asked to do on a regular basis. Indeed it was probably a dangerous place to be, alone with his thoughts with nothing to preoccupy him.

It wasn't unusual to be given an assignment where he didn't know all the details but it was strange to him that his orders required him to sit in a public place and wait for the action to unfold in front of him. Then when he knew all he heard from his hopefully unsuspecting victim, he would strike as soon as the enemy was alone and eliminate him.

To kill in cold blood wasn't alien to him either: it was what had got him to where he was today.

He possessed a headstrong, determined character and his hair was as black as the night and a possessed a poker face to match his strong, assertive features. He was the perfect man for the job.

He glanced at the clock again. 10:10.

Suddenly, the bell above the door to the restaurant jangled into life. The man in the corner looked up. The person he had been waiting for walked through the door with three associates, all in professional clothing, masked by long coats that kept the harsh winter wind out. The men all wore friendly faces, pleasantly joking between themselves as they handed they're coats to the waiter.

The setting for such a duel was unnerving for the man watching, there were at least half a dozen people enjoying their meals in the restaurant and he knew he had to pick the right moment – otherwise he would be spending the rest of the day sitting in a dank cell, waiting for his superior to bail him out. It would tarnish his good reputation as the best assassin in the business. But what good is an assassin who gets caught in a public place. *Maybe this was a test?*, he thought to himself as his eyes stalked the party of men across the room.

The man in the corner sat watching the party settle down at the round table opposite him. He had to be casual yet focused on his work, and decided to tuck in to his bacon and eggs on Italian bread and act just like any other person in the restaurant. The once piping hot meal would have to be eaten otherwise it would arouse suspicion that a well dressed man was sitting by himself with a full plate of food in front of him that was untouched. He didn't want to hand the advantage to his prey. They weren't the kind of people you would want to show your hand too.

As the soggy bacon entered his mouth he listened intensively to the conversation at the opposite table. He had registered the men's features as they entered. His had been drawn to his main target. His ONLY target. The others were to live, according to his superior. Carefully, the man in the corner studied the profile of a man he knew as "The Boss." He was a plump man, in his late fifties, clean-shaven with eyes like a boar and a toupee balanced unconvincingly on his domed head.

The tallest member of the party was his son. The complete opposite to his father, he stood a proud foot over his Dad - slim with a short haircut - confident in his speech.

11

The other two looked like bodyguards, well built and thuggish, like they had walked out of a film about gangsters in the East End. The jovial banter between the foursome ceased and they were deep in discussion. As the man in the corner finished his mouthful, he heard the plot unfold.

'With the funds that both myself and my associate are willing to accept from you, your empire will be safe for now. It seems such a pity that so many men had to suffer for us to get this far, but I am grateful that you and your heir finally agreed to the deal,' said one of the heavies, speaking in a calm yet assertive tone.

It was clear to the man in the corner that the pleasantries expressed when they arrived at the restaurant were only for appearances sake - so that they did not arouse suspicion. For now they could get down to business.

The restaurant was loud enough for them to air their dirty washing in public without people hearing, yet just audible for the man to listen to. But, why come to somewhere like this in broad daylight? The man in the corner found this curious. He felt a burning sensation in the back of his head, telling him that something was wrong...

It was also a good thing that he did that deal with the waiter to sit them at that table. Now if only the dictaphone taped to the underside of the table went unnoticed, he knew the trap was still set.

'I can assure you those men you speak of were nothing to do with me,' replied The Boss. 'Then again with a history like mine another drop of blood isn't a reason to cry over spilt milk.'

He continued. 'I have been running the firm for over 30 years now. I had hoped that one day I could hand my good work over to my lad and after all the history we two families have had, it was important to me to make sure he was well set up and if that meant doing a deal with you lot, then so be it.'

He put his hand reassuringly on his sons arm.

'We welcome an alliance, especially if this last job you do means that both of us can retire to sunny climates away from the filth in this shitty country,' the heavy retorted.

His superior had told the man in the corner about a job, yet it still surprised him that they were doing it in such a public manner.

Maybe it was because they knew that the sharks were already swimming around they're offices in the city and with all the enemies both parties had made, at least in this place they couldn't be harmed.

The man chuckled to himself.

Poor, unsuspecting fools.

13

The conversation continued. 'So, half of the 20 million will be transferred to your Monaco account by Wednesday. Then the rest will be raised after the job on the piggy bank,' explained the son, his arrogance shining through his weak tones. It was obvious to the man in the corner that he was someone who hid behind his father and clearly never did the dirty work. Like a bully's associate at school, the son was the one who held the coats and laughed at the thug's jokes to feel a part of the crowd. *Coward*, thought the man in the corner.

'All we need now is assurance that my father here will be given immunity from the Big Chief. We all know that a run in with him would end up with us up on hooks.'
The three men nodded.

'At least with both our companies joining forces there will be double the effort and manpower just in case he DOES attack,' assured the second heavy.

The man in the corner braved another mouthful of his depressing meal.

This was the information he wanted. So there would be an attack, but where? Also who was the Big Chief?

Was that the man he was working for? Could it be that these firms were really talking about his superior at the Secret Service? He tried to block the questions out of his mind and continued to spy on the party.

14

'So, the deal is done then, the job with commence at 12.30 in two days time,' The Boss declared. 'What we will need is plastic explosives to get into the vault and enough manpower to throw muscle around just in case anyone in the vault is stupid enough to get in our way. I haven't got where I am today by taking kindly to people who think that saving the day will earn them a pat on the back from the authorities or an easy shag with their colleague and nobody is going to stop me from paying my debts, starting a new life and making sure my firm -'

'OUR firms,' interrupted the first heavy.

'Of course,' continued The Boss, '- OUR firms are set up for the future and strong enough to fend off any attack, especially from the Big Chief.'

So, it was fear that had made the target want to broker the deal, thought the man in the corner.

He had to endure one last big party before disappearing with last of the millions of pounds of blood money he earned through illegal means over the decades. Basically he was doing a runner before the sharks came and tore him to pieces.

The man in the corner now had everything he needed, except for the final details about the Big Chief that both these villainous families were cowering from.

For the moment that was unimportant he had to tell himself.
Today is about one thing and one thing only.

Taking out The Boss.

'So it is settled, let's order some grub and toast our hopefully long and successful marriage,' The Boss enthused, holding out his hand to shake with his new partner.

'I'm happy to be bringing these two families together,' grinned the first heavy, who took The Boss' hand and shook it vigorously.

'Right, I'll have today's special and I'll see you in a minute, got to go drop the kids off at the pool first! Make mine a large one Harry,' The Boss pushed his way past his associates and patted his beaming son on the shoulder.

As he walked towards the restroom, the man in the corner knew that this was his chance. He would have to hope and pray that nobody else was in the toilets with them otherwise he would have the police on his back and two angry firm leaders to deal with, not to mention a grieving and vengeful son – no matter how weak and ineffective he seemed.

The Boss failed to notice his assassin sitting at the table and walked into the small room. Less than ten seconds later, the man in the corner left his lonely table and joined him.

The man surveyed the room. White porcelain urinals lined the wall while clean sinks and judging mirrors adorned the other. Right in front of him was a row of four, blank cream-coloured cubicles. He walked slowly towards them, his eyes darting left and right, checking the locks on the doors. Only one was locked. His victim was trapped.

As he approached the cubicle he was repulsed by the noises the heard in there. He did, however, take comfort in the fact that this man was about to die in his own filth. *A fitting end to a nasty piece of work*, he thought.

His footsteps were barely audible, since his size ten boots had a rubber heel and didn't make a sound on the harsh carpet flooring. The Boss began to whistle to himself, occasionally grunting with every bowel movement.

The man from the corner took it as a chance to take his gun from his inside pocket. He was handed further luck when the boss started to hum loudly.

The Times They Are A-Changing by Bob Dylan.

At least this old bastard has some taste, the man from the corner thought as he took the chance to fit the silencer barrel to his pistol. His breathing calm and steady, the man began to raise his gun to just above the lock, around half way across the door.

This was it.

17

His heart thumping rapidly against his ribcage, the moment had come.

His pulse bruising his eardrums, his inner calmness was now awash with adrenaline. Then a sound made him jump. It wasn't the toilet door opening; it was The Boss breaking into full song.

The impromptu blast from the cubicle was followed by a small one from the barrel of the pistol.

The man from the corner had shot clean through the door with pinpoint precision. A small hole had formed in the cubicle door and the singing had stopped.

The man from the corner looked through his handiwork to see The Boss, looking as surprised as a rabbit in the headlights, trousers around his ankles in a most un-dignified pose.

A small trickle of blood began to ooze through the hole that had burrowed in the middle of the forehead and his bulky figure began to slide off the throne of defecation and smacked with a deathly thud against the cubicle door.

The man from the corner began to dismantle his weapon and hide it neatly in his inside pocket.

He wiped a tiny bead of sweat from his brow and backed away from the door. The times they are a-changing?

18

'Yes, for the better,' said the assassin to no-one in particular as he turned on his heels and left the murder scene.

If he had looked over his shoulder at the place of his victim's demise he would have seen a small pool of blood begin to form at the base of the cubicle door.

As the man returned to the main restaurant he would have to improvise to get his Dictaphone out without arousing suspicion. He grabbed his things when he noticed a waiter approaching The Boss' table with four drinks on a tray.

The man from the corner pretended to grapple awkwardly with his coat and bag when he knocked into the waiter, knocking both themselves and the drinks onto the floor. He rolled under the feet of the three men waiting for their fourth member to return.

In all of the confusion and since he had caused the men to stand up, he grabbed for the dictaphone, ripping it from its secure bonds and in a flash whipped it into his top pocket where it nestled with his murder weapon.

'Oi! What the bloody hell do you think you are doing!' shouted the son, who looked down damningly on the man from the corner.

'I'm so sorry, I cannot apologize enough, let me help you up,' he extended his arm to the flattened waiter, who was looking dumbstruck.

'Let me pay for your meal.'

'Nah, don't worry mate, I'd watch out if I were you though, clumsy men don't tend to last long in this area,' the son was trying to look big in front of his new business partners but the man from the corner knew he could crush his puny frame with one blow to the nose.

'It won't happen again,' he said maintaining eye contact with the juvenile.

With that, the man from the corner had bought himself enough time to pay the bill, which he did in cash after he had created enough confusion to slip out into the chilly, cold day and away from the aftershock of what he had just committed.

Within three minutes he had completed his mission, obtained the information both he and his superior needed and escaped, albeit making a scene in the process.

He knew his act was necessary to retrieve the vital evidence of what the two newly wedded firms were plotting.

As he wheeled down the busy street and pulled his warm welcoming coat over his taut frame, the man from the corner was imagining the reaction when the boss' undignified fate was discovered by his associates.

He took great pleasure in bringing down one of the most hated criminals in the country.

His superior would be proud. Maybe he would get a pay rise for his work? The thought raced through his mind as he with a brisk pace away from the restaurant.

Yet, certain details in the conversation still puzzled him.

Who was this so-called 'Big Chief' and why had he never heard of him? This dark fable he had heard over a breakfast table – a man whose very name could make men of blood and violence quake in their boots?

This was something that the unknown man was going to have to find out.

CHAPTER TWO

BLOOD FOG

The city is the perfect place for hiding your dirty deeds. It is big enough to keep your sins away from judging eyes and full of people who don't bat an eyelid if they hear an ambulance or police car on a regular basis.

Sirens, noise and smoke are just as much of the make-up of the place as the smog and clouds, which hold it in a gloomy fog.

You could even voice your plans of death and destruction in a public place and nobody would hear. Well, that was what one group of men had thought.

It had been two months since the leader of one organisation - The Boss - had been killed in the toilet cubicle of an uptown restaurant. His son, Harry, the heir to The Boss' throne, had found his body, soaked in a pool of his own blood, naked from the waist down with a hole in the middle of his forehead.

Harry, in a blind state of panic, thought that his two associates - who were from a rival gang trying to broker an alliance to keep both parties safe – had killed his beloved father, and he turned a gun that he had hid on his person on the men.

This had led the workers at the restaurant to restrain him until he was arrested, for what the authorities saw as the murder of his father.

Before the police arrived, the two men disappeared, leaving a poor grief-stricken Harry confused and facing accusations of murder.

When the police questioned him, and carried out an autopsy on The Boss, they soon realised that this wasn't their man, yet the arrest had led to further enquiries into The Boss' former dealings.

Harry was released, but now the authorities were aware of his firm and the scent was rank with unsolved crimes going back over a quarter of a century.

The first thing Harry did was get the family lawyer, a man by the name of Mr. Bryce, to get working on a case that would cleared his name and make sure that he wasn't made to pay for the blood spilt in the past.

Next he tracked down the two men, from an organisation called GEMINI, who he insisted on meeting.

There were too many questions to ask and since the deal hadn't gone through and the job wasn't completed, they now probably wanted his head too.

It was going to be dangerous, so he decided to make the setting a nice quiet one, and he'd need to take his best men, just in case it turned nasty.

The old warehouse his dad used to own, the one he was taken to regularly as a boy, would do.

Then there was the big one, perhaps the question he wanted to know most of all. Who was the man in the corner of the restaurant?

The man who had caused that commotion by falling into their table and whose eyes had seemed cold and deadly?

Who was this man who had killed his father?

The meeting date was set, February 4th, 22:00, at the disused warehouse on Brambly Road.

The backdrop was dark and un-nerving. The showdown was yet to begin.

Harry looked up at the sky from the back seat of his Mercedes as it glided along the city's puddle-ridden streets.

The night was as dark as the rings that hung heavily under his youthful eyes.

He hadn't slept much since his father's assassination, and the strain of running a dead man's business all by himself was taking a toll.

Deep down, he knew he was far too young to be in such a perilous position.

At twenty-two, he should be out with his friends, chasing tail and indulging in the pleasures the world offers a young man such as himself.

The money that his dad bought home was both a blessing and a curse, he thought to himself. It meant that he got into all the best clubs, mostly because The Boss owned the bouncers who worked at them, and his playboy lifestyle of booze, guns, sex with multiple partners, and the fear his father brought to local criminals had shielded him from the anxieties of real life.

Now that shield had gone, and he was staring fear right in the face.

His mind ceased wandering and he looked around the car. There were three other men accompanying him. They were your stereotypical-looking gangsters, built like broad tree trunks and attired in dark leather clothing.

These men made Harry feel safe, for now.   He knew that tonight could be the making or the breaking of him.

26

'We're nearly there, son,' said the driver, twisting his head away from the road towards his boss adjacent to him. 'Shouldn't we park up quite close to the exit just in case it turns ugly?'

Harry hadn't thought of that. 'Yes, of course Dev, let the others know will yer? Strength in numbers.'

He nodded towards the radio that had been installed in the car.

The man sitting in the passenger seat, a heavy with the nickname 'Bowser' picked the microphone up in his bearlike hands.

'We're gonna park up at the exit around back,' he barked. 'Remember to load your insurance before we go inside.'

Harry scanned his brain for what the word 'insurance' had meant. He was so nervous a trickle of sweat had fallen off his chin onto the tie that was fastened tightly around his collared neck.

'No worries boss,' assured Bowser, 'These bastards won't touch ya if we have our wits about us.'

He turned back to the front of the car without a reassuring smile. Harry breathed hard; two more streets to go.

He dug his fingers into the leather upholstery either side of him and closed his eyes tight.

Composure was the key ingredient tonight.

The car swerved off the busy street down an alley, which led to the back of the disused warehouse. It looked quiet enough; nobody in his, or her, right minds would be wandering down here tonight.

As the car came to a halt outside the exit doors, the rain started.

Thick, heavy rain.

Puddles splashed as two more Mercedes pulled up next to Harry's car. The entourage was complete.

With one final hard breath, Harry opened the car door and stepped out into the wet night, in unison with the other men in the cars.

Another eight men emerged from their vehicles, all the same black Mercedes model. *A twelve-man-strong unit, well it was better to be safe than sorry*, thought Harry.

He took a look at all of them: all double his age and far more experienced than he was.

'Right, let's do this,' he stammered, before leading his men through the exit doors and into the dark, dank warehouse.

*

The warehouse had been derelict for nearly ten years. The Boss ran his cover-up firm, Taylor Industries, from here. It was a paper manufacturing venture and it worked as a cover for his dodgy dealings both financially and physically, when he had punished the people who had either betrayed him or threatened his
empire.

God how Harry wished his father were here right now.

He'd show these GEMINI pricks a thing or two! The entourage moved through a pitch-black entrance lobby before they ventured into the main hall.

The place stank of rotting wood and of terrible deeds of old.

When the gang had assembled in the vast room, Harry looked through the dark nervously.

'Somebody put the facking lights on,' he spat. Dev felt along the harsh brick wall and flicked the switch.

The lights stuttered into life, hanging from a metal gantry, which was still in total darkness.

Looking up as his eyes adjusted to the bright light that began to wash the room, Harry felt uneasy at what may lurk beyond the lights in the darkness.

He heard the cocking of guns all around him, which made him twitch. Adjusting his eyes to look straight in front of him, he focused on the two figures that stood in front of the thug

29

army. It was the men who had sat with him in the restaurant on that terrible day.

All of a sudden, his tired eyes became flushed with anger.

There stood the two men from GEMINI.

'Whoa, what's with all the metal work?' said the first man, holding his hands up in defence. 'We were under the impression that we were just going to have a little talk?'

'Bollocks,' cried Harry, his fists clenched with rage. 'You know the real reason why we're here!'

The man looked puzzled, and pursed his lips in thought.

'Nope,' he replied.

'It was you two who got me arrested for my dad's killing, and then you fled the scene and left me to pick up the pieces. We've had the pigs snooping around for two months, while you lot didn't hold up your side of the bargain and haven't given us any protection: where the hell have you been?!'

'But we were under the impression that the deal was off, you never carried out the job on the bank and both our firms are still as vulnerable from the Big Chief as they were before your old man got done,' said the second GEMINI member, whose heavy build contradicted his blonde hair and cool tones.

This new information soothed Harry's mind, but didn't deter him from his anger.

'I could have squealed, I could have told the old plods that there was this gang of criminals called GEMINI who have been stealing, killing and trying to prize this city out of my dad's hands for years without success.'

Harry could feel the adrenaline flooding his veins.

'Look, kid, can we have an adult conversation without all of the guns and shouting?' said the first man, who's good-looking African features and sharp suit made him look like a prince among men.

Harry looked to his left and right. His gang's guns were still loaded and pointed at the GEMINI men.

He made a gesture with his hands as if to tell the men to stand easy.

'Good, that's much better,' said the heavy, who then sat down on a crate.

'Right let's get one thing clear, we met with your father and yourself to broker a deal to keep both our companies afloat: let's face it, these waters have been infested with big sharks for ages and we can't swim alone anymore.

Now, we were only going to enter this marriage if your old man carried out the job on the bank, then that money would have helped pay his debts and for us to join together, meaning he could retire knowing that your future was in good hands.'

31

'But why would he trust you anyway? Why, after all these years of fighting to keep you away?' asked Harry, who was trying to keep cool, but the pain of his father's loss made his voice break with emotion.

The heavy leaned forward, locking eyes with the young man. 'Because your father knew that there is something much bigger and badder out there than us, which can crush both of our companies with one blow.'

This sentence made Harry gulp hard. His father had told him that there was some kind of organisation out there that was so dangerous that he strived to stay out of their business.

Maybe that was why this so-called 'Big Chief' had The Boss killed? Maybe there was something he knew that he should never have been allowed to know.

'So,' Harry shook as he spoke, 'They had my father killed?' The heavy didn't reply to him. He stared blankly back at the boy, silent.

'ANSWER ME!' screamed Harry, his cry echoing around the big hall.

A few more seconds passed before the man from GEMINI spoke again. 'You need to ask yourself a very, very serious question,' he answered.

The other GEMINI member moved away from his colleague and towards a door opposite the one Harry and his men had come in through.

'Your firm was dying; it was sick. It was down to the skin and bone of what it was and why was that? Was it because your men were dying off? Was it because they were getting sent to the Old Bailey? NO! It was because your father had no one else to trust and knew that enlisting any more thugs could result in a mole in the company.'

Harry stared at the man from GEMINI, his eyes welling with tears.

He readied his gun, levelling it at the man who was advancing towards him slowly with his hands behind his back.

'Now, the question is: what if that mole had already burrowed his way in and was using what he knew as a way of protecting all he had and was reporting back to the Big Chief?

What if that mole had been there all along, and years of alliance and trust with the Big Man was then betrayed, and then that little mole began to dig away scared that he would be the next head on a spike?'

The heavy was by this point just a couple of inches away from the young man's emotion-filled face. 'What if...your old man...WAS that mole?'

33

'NO!' hollered Harry, spit dripping from his teeth, tears streaming down his face. His father had betrayed him all these years. The man he looked up to, so cruelly taken away from him, was a grass.

He was trying to save his own sorry arse and had landed his inexperienced young son right in the thick of it.

He cocked his handgun and began to squeeze the trigger.

BANG!

The sound of gunfire shot through the air and bounced around the auditorium. It made the ground shake and some of Harry's men jumped like little girls.

It even stopped the second GEMINI man from his advance on the other door, where backup lurked in case of a shoot-out situation.

The first man from GEMINI stood with a look of shock on his face. His eyes staring at the young man whose face had turned from one of anguish to one of pain.

As both he and the gang stood aghast at Harry - the man who would be king of his own empire, so young and so betrayed by his darling father, slumped to the ground, dead.

For a few seconds the criminals stood in absolute silence at the prone body. There was a bullet entry hole that pierced the top of his back and his organs had exploded outward onto the crisp suit of the GEMINI representative.

He lay in an ever-increasing pool of blood. Face down on the floor, a look of agony and surprise on his face.

All the men in the room were thinking the same thing. That shot had come from the ceiling.

'You bastard!' shouted Bowser.

The man from GEMINI was still in shock.

'I...no...I...'

'Kill him!' The gang readied their guns, just as a shot from the other side of the hall caught Dev in the shoulder.

The man who had been staring Harry in the face, who now had his guts pasted to his suit, dived for cover behind some nearby crates. The gang took up similar positions and sent a hail of bullets towards where that bullet had come from. GEMINI gang members had used the moment of surprise to set themselves up and begin an attack on Harry's men.

The battle was now on. The sound of bullets rang around the vast room, filling it with the sound of death. Cold, sharp metal began to pierce the skin of men on both sides.

The man covered in Harry's blood edged his way towards the door that led to a staircase.

Bowser noticed his retreat and fired his shotgun at him.

One blast from his gun buried itself in the wall about four inches above his head and the man was able to fire back, forcing Bowser to cover.

Soon though, the sound of bullets and grown men screaming curdled in the warehouse.

The man from GEMINI grabbed his chance and dived through the doorway to safety. He backed against the wall in the dark at the foot of the stairs and caught his breath, still shocked at what had happened.

After a few moments he glanced to his left and saw the exit sign. He had to get out and report back on the madness that had occurred.

He had only taken a couple of steps when someone kicked his gun clean out of his hand, startling him.

Before he had a chance to retaliate, this mystery man delivered a right-hook hard into his rib cage, winding the GEMINI man who, as he arched his back in a natural reaction to the blow, received another one - this time a knee to his chin, which sent him flying back onto the hard floor.

Dazed, with his body flowing with pain, the mystery man muttered to his victim, 'Get up!' he ordered, picking the man up by the scruff of his already ruined suit and forcing him up the metal stairs.

Every step aided the pain that the man was experiencing in his ribcage and on his jaw. He could feel both beginning to swell.

His jaw felt like it was protruding forward like a comedy mask. He lost count of how many flights of stairs he was forced up, and was on the verge of blacking out when he felt the cold rain patter on his damaged face.

The unknown man had dragged his victim up six flights of stairs and pushed him through the half open door, which enveloped onto the roof.

The floor was sodden, flooding from the heavy rain that continued to cascade down upon them.

The man from GEMINI coughed as he tried to get up. His vision, blurry from his ordeal, began to caress the outline of the man who had so suddenly attacked him.

He recognised him, but from where? The sound of gunshots was still audible even from this height. The sound of death bled all the way up the building to the roof. The unknown man began to speak.

'Now while your friends are having a little party down there, I thought that we could have one of our own,' he said in an eloquent yet icy tone. 'I've been watching you boys from GEMINI for a while and I know that you are far too well stocked to be dealing with that spotty nerd.'

37

The man from GEMINI had got up to his feet. Straightening his posture, his voice was dry as he replied, 'How do you know that I am from GEMINI? We are a secret organization.'

'I have my ways,' the unknown man retorted.   'Two months ago both you and The Boss were formalising a deal to protect you from someone you referred to as 'Big Chief': I want to know who that is and where you fit into the picture.'

The GEMINI agent laughed. 'Only one man could possibly know that. It's you, isn't it? You're the man in the corner. You killed The Boss and then finished his son off tonight, didn't you? Was it really worth it to end a dying firm?'

The unknown man stared blankly at his captive.

'If you want to cure the cancer first you have to cut out the tumours.'

'Oh, and I suppose I am your next target?' The agent pointed at himself. 'You see, I don't think you have a clue what you are getting yourself into – let's see, a rogue agent? A man seeking vengeance or a man just doing his job? Or am I right in all of the above?'

The GEMINI man began to laugh again when his captor launched at him grabbing him by the throat and dragging him to the edge of the roof.   Gasping for air, the agent began to claw at his face and arm to let go.

'I'm giving you your final warning,' whispered the unknown man. 'You will give me a name now or I will feed you to the pavement below, it's your choice.'

'Okay. Okay!" gasped the man from GEMINI. 'But I will only tell you if it means that you are after the big man himself.' The unknown man nodded.

'I'll give you a name and where you can find her.'

Her? The mention of a female caught the unknown man off-guard. Maybe it was because, in this brutal world of his, it was mainly the male of the species he had been assigned to kill. This threw him into all kinds of different waters.

'Her name is Michelle Alison Simmons,' the agent croaked through his exasperated larynx. 'I am meant to be meeting her at the Café Montague tomorrow at nine. She will give you all the information that you need, but God help you man, because he knows who you are, he knows and he will hunt you down like the dog that you are!'

The unknown man had heard enough. He let go of the agent's throat and pushed him away.

The momentum carried the agent back and he tripped on the ledge. In desperation, the man from GEMINI clawed at the unknown man, shouting for him to help.

All that he did though was watch, as the man fell over the edge of the warehouse roof and onto the deserted alleyway below.

His screams sent a shiver into the night, and the sound of the impact of bone and ligament on concrete was sickening. But the unknown man didn't bat an eyelid.

He turned away from the ledge, and started towards the door leading back into the warehouse. The gunfire had stopped. Time to see if the coast was clear.

As he stepped onto the gantry from where he had shot Harry, the unknown man glared down onto the devastation of what he had created below.

A blood fog seemed to hang above the bodies of both Harry's men and the men from GEMINI who also lay slain.

The unknown man allowed himself to feel the shame of his work for a few seconds.

True, these were the goons who worked for the scum who ran this country, but the real people who did the dirty work were probably sitting in their fancy houses on the money they had made from the deaths of innocent and manipulated people over the years.

If he paused from time-to-time, the unknown man was repulsed by his job and what he was asked to do by his

40

superior. Maybe the old fart should come and get some blood on his hands every once in a while.

He counted the corpses. Everybody who he had counted on entering the building lay dead down below him.

He sighed long and hard as he picked up his sniper gun and folded it away neatly into his suitcase.

As he climbed off the gantry he thought to himself of how the authorities would find this one out. *Probably some poor kids playing in the area would notice something was up, poor little buggers.*

He decided that he would leave an anonymous tip when he was clear of the warehouse, so the innocent remained out of the picture.

The unknown man made his way quietly down the metal stairwell, his sopping clothes dripping on the old metal. He shuddered when he realised that he was in a big abandoned warehouse full of corpses.

It was the stuff of nightmares. Would it affect how much sleep he would get tonight? Probably. But then again, sleep was one of the only pleasures he had remaining nowadays.

He pondered whether this so-called 'Big Chief' did know who he really was? No. It was probably just an idle threat from the human pizza on the alleyway.

When he got to the foot of the stairs the unknown man could barely bring himself to peer into the main hall and glimpse at the devastation and waste of human life. He looked away quickly and with a gloved hand slowly turned the lights off.

As he stepped outside, he respectfully shut the exit door and looked at the three impressive Mercedes cars that sat waiting for their passengers who would never return.

He paused for a moment, questioning whether to steal one of them. It was probably for the best if he left them, otherwise his superior would be left wondering why he would endanger this whole operation by stealing a car. He took his black gloves, stuffed them in his soaking coat pocket and walked away from the warehouse of death, never looking back and towards the main street, which was 300 yards away.

'Well,' he said to himself 'I'd better grab myself an early night; I've got a date tomorrow evening.'

CHAPTER THREE

DANCING WITH THE DEVIL

9.15pm

Café Montague

Michelle Alison Simmons was waiting patiently for her partner to arrive. It wasn't like Toby to be late. She hadn't heard from him all day and this had her worried.

Of course, being a guy he was probably just doing it for effect, trying to scare her a little and force her to reveal how much she cared for his well-being when he did show up. *Cheek*, thought Michelle, she had played the game too long to be taken for an innocent fool like that. Her fringe of raven black hair bobbed in front of her forehead as her head collapsed into her cupped hands. She was waiting for her man

43

to return to her with information regarding the situation with Harry Seymour and his crumbling empire.

He had told her about the deal that had fallen through with his father, The Boss, and that he and his business partner were meeting with the young man to sort the mess out once and for all.   When she spoke to the man from GEMINI on the phone, he used the words 'sort it out' – and that could only mean one thing. Death. But for whom? Was he intentionally late or had something very bad happened during that meeting?

On the business side of things, it would be detrimental to the plans of the Big Chief if GEMINI had been wiped out, but not fatal. On the personal side, it could mean the end of blossoming relationship.

The girl looked at her watch again. 9:17. She sighed hard and looked around her at the other customers in the flash restaurant. Couples wining and dining. Some looked like they were on dates, young and innocent with not so innocent designs for how the night might end.

Then there were the 'older and wiser' husband and wife pairings with their eyes full of hurt and deceit. How Michelle pitied them. Who'd want to end up like that?

'I take it that this seat isn't taken?'

Michelle jumped at the surprise guest at her table. She looked up at the figure that now stood in front of her, his hands clasped to the chair.

The man was well built, in his early thirties and was dressed in a dark shirt and trousers, blending in to the night from which he had come. Michelle's eyes met with his. Hers, dark green and soft, his, cold and puppy dog blue.

His face was lined from years of tense exertions and it told her that this was a man who was not to be trusted.

'Not at all,' she replied.

The unknown man dragged the chair back, its hind legs screeching on the floor. He then sat on the chair dragging it forward: the screeching made Michelle wince. She half expected this mystery man to drag the chair elsewhere but he sat directly in front of her.

He had maintained eye contact during his manoeuvre and sat staring at the girl in front of him.

She's not as young as she looks, thought the unknown man. She must have been in her late twenties. She looked innocent enough but there was something under her skin that made him think that she had seen too much for her age.

'Well, you certainly know how to make an entrance,' said Michelle. 'Do you normally approach girls who sit by themselves in cafes?'

45

'I try not to make a habit of it,' replied the man. He had barely blinked since he joined Michelle at her table for two.

'Well, as you can see,' she continued, 'someone has beaten you to the post; looks like you'll have to find another lonely lady somewhere else.'

The unknown man put his hand in his left trouser pocket and took out a wallet. He opened it and placed it on the table, facing his companion.

The drivers' licence showed through the clear plastic on the outside of the wallet, showing a picture of a handsome African face and the name Toby Smith.

Michelle's eyes grew hard; she gulped and looked into her companion's eyes.

'Something tells me he won't be coming,' said the man, holding back a smirk.

'How did he die?' asked Michelle as she chewed on her cheek nervously.

'Uncomfortably. Funny really, I thought something like that would have made the papers by now. "Gang lord found dead." I'm surprised that you didn't know; then again, maybe they couldn't identify the body with no identification on his person.'

Michelle felt sick. The appetite she had been building up throughout the day was now all but vanquished.

She was sharing a table with the man who had killed her counterpart.

The chance to build on that relationship Toby had had all but gone now too. Michelle looked hard at the mystery man in his place.

'What are you doing here?' The colour had washed from Michelle's already pale features and she could barely bring herself to look at the murderer in front of her.

'The same reason as you,' replied the unknown man. 'I have been following the activities of all the crime syndicates in this country for the last two years. Along the way I have come across some of the very scum of this world and found myself here, the epicentre of the sewage that flows through the veins of our nation. As my research has continued, I have found out that all of the gangs, drug lords, pimps, fat cats and club owners are all run by the same person; I want some information and I want it now.'

Of course, it was all becoming clear to Michelle now.

This was the man.

The man without an identity. The man who had tailored his whole being to become a ruthless, cold hearted and manic. He was the assassin she had been told to avoid.

'Who is the Big Chief?'

Michelle chuckled, at first softly, then loud enough for the few neighbouring tables to hear.

The unknown man knew what she was up to.

She was making as much noise to draw the attention to them and alert people in the café of his presence. He looked around intently.

Michelle's violent laughs turned into a sharp exhale. 'For someone who has committed so much time to your obsession it must hurt that you still don't have a clue who the Big Chief is?'

The unknown man was shocked. This girl had gone from feeling moved about her companion's death to being just as cold and hard as he was.

Who was she?

'You shoes are awfully small from where I'm sitting, you shouldn't try playing with the big boys' darling, you might get burnt.'

Despite his threat, the unknown man did not see any weakness in her eyes.

'Why were you meeting with GEMINI?'

'Okay, since your homework isn't up to scratch but you have shown your working out, I'll help you with the answers,' she relented. Anyway, what she was about to say wouldn't damage her plans.

'GEMINI is a corporation run by two brothers. The man who you killed and another. The star sign that bonds them is obviously Gemini. One black, one white. One a little on the lazy side, one hard working. Together they began running a business of debt collectors in this city around thirty years ago.'

She paused to take a sip from her untouched red wine.

'Around the same time, a man by the name of Neville Seymour, who ran a factory on Brambly Road, also began to collect money off those who were far more deserving than him. He also ran a club called Inferno, where after one in the morning after the public had gone home, it would turn into a brothel for his paying clients. Slowly he built an empire, and got a big head in the process, making his workers and punters call him "The Boss."'

'The GEMINI twins noticed that he was beginning to step on their turf. A quarter of a century of blackmail and murder began, with far too many people getting caught in the crossfire.'

'So, why did they decide to broker a deal? If there was no love lost between them then why were they trying to make a deal to unite?' The man probed the girls face. She wasn't telling any lies.

'There was one encounter, about ten years ago, when both companies met for a battle in a warehouse. They were posing

49

as football hooligans, so when the police found the mess it just looked like two teams had got over-excited and done each other in. For GEMINI though, it was a disaster.

Both of the firms' leaders were killed. The Boss had taken the upper hand, but he was unaware that they had sons who were able to step into their father's boots.'

She took another swig of her wine and licked her thick, luscious lips before she started again. The waiter approached the table with two menus, but the unknown man waved him away like a wasp hovering with intent over a picnic hamper.

'The sons swore revenge on The Boss and spent half a decade ruining him. First they took away his factory, the backbone to his empire. The sons placed moles inside the company then the next thing, money was going missing. Within a matter of months, Inferno was closed due to a drugs bust, leading to the exposure of the prostitution ring and putting The Boss in prison for a year. When he came out, he found out that his men had had their heads turned by GEMINI and his money was all but gone.'

'So, he started to gamble to get his wealth back,' interrupted the unknown man.

Michelle nodded. 'As you probably know, gambling wasn't his strong point: breaking arms was.'

50

The unknown man agreed. 'He played poker like it was a game of snap. No technique and not a clue.'

'He was so far in debt that he started doing favours for those who he once owned,' Michelle was surprised at how little the man across the table from her knew. Surely he already knew what she was telling him?

'The final insult was to sell his soul to GEMINI in exchange for their help on a big bank job,' she continued.

'He also wanted to leave his son, Harry, with a leg to stand on, although I've heard that his lifestyle was also a huge drain on his father's finances.'

'You've missed something out,' the unknown man pointed in the direction of the strong female. 'He was scared of something, or someone. He wasn't doing the job so that he could rebuild his empire, he was doing it so he had enough to start a new life somewhere else; what link does he have to the Big Chief?'

Michelle searched for an answer. 'Maybe he owed him money?'

'No, he had worked for the Big Chief in the past. I heard that he was somebody who did the dirty work for the Big Chief occasionally. I heard that he was a snitch too.'

'Possibly, it was probably safer to obey the Big Chief to start with – only as time went on he became more tangled in the web and couldn't get out.'

'Joining GEMINI was degrading enough, but being exposed as a grass, that's worse than death.' Michelle then eyed her dark stranger up and began her assault. 'Now it's your turn,' she whispered. 'I know who you are; you don't scare me with all of this ambiguity and mystery. It was you who killed The Boss and now you have destroyed GEMINI too; was it worth it?'

'Well, it led me to you,' the unknown man smiled. 'What's your link with GEMINI?'

'I was dating Toby until his accident,' she sighed.

'Don't take me for a fool. You know far too much to be just a trophy girlfriend. You're Michelle Alison Simmons, personal assistant to a politician called Sir Michael Houghton who is Chief Liaison with the Metropolitan Police, You are far more than just a girl with big tits and you're up to your neck in it.'

'You've noticed…maybe I shouldn't have helped you with your homework,' retorted Michelle. 'Have you been looking over other pupil's shoulders?'

The unknown man was losing his patience fast. 'I know that your boss is up to his neck in this; one of the corrupt pigs whose benefitting from all of this mess. What is his connection to the Big Chief? No cheap shots and don't flutter your eyelashes at me hun, I'm immune.'

Michelle smiled and lent in towards the unknown man 'Well, regardless of whether you are immune or not, you can't touch me. Don't think that blackmail will get you your answers. Sir Michael knows nothing of my part in all of this and it would be unwise to suggest it.' The unknown man's blood began to boil.

He wasn't going to be made to keep silent over this.

'I still don't think you know what kind of danger you have got your pretty little head into.' He leaned forward too, hoping that she would retreat back. She didn't.

'Oh no, I don't think you know what *you* are getting yourself into,' he was now so close to her that he could smell her last cigarette on her breath.

'Besides, we wouldn't want you to get hurt now would we?'

The unknown man could feel the rage beginning to flow through his being.

This web was becoming more and more tangled. If this lady had been one of the goons he had been hunting down she would now be dead. He had a gun in his jacket pocket and the urge to use it was rising.

'I'm giving you your last warning,' the unknown man's eyes were now filling with anger. Michelle knew that if she didn't get out soon, he could do it.

Her safety wasn't completely guaranteed.

After all, he had wiped out two pawns in the Big Chief's chess set. He was cheating in this game, making illegal moves and now she knew what he looked like, the Big Chief could have him hunted down and wiped out.

Nobody had crossed the Big Chief yet so why should some cheap upstart want to do it now?

'Either you tell me who the Big Chief is or I will end your existence.' The unknown man glared at Michelle. Another drop of blood on his hands to wipe the city clean, he thought.

'Okay, check.' Michelle was still untried by the threats of the killer opposite her.

'The Big Chief has been at the top of the tree for decades. He controls everything, just like you said. But you do not understand just how deeply rooted he is in the make-up of this city. The Big Chief is the ruler of every single living soul. His empire controls the Government, the hospitals, the churches, the bankers, the liars, the cheaters and every innocent person who lives here.

Nobody is safe once the Big Chief is crossed. That's why your friend The Boss was living in fear. He had unfinished business with the Big Man and his punishment was death.'

A nasty thought occurred to the unknown man. Was that the reason why he had been sent to kill that vile little man? He knew there was something up when he was handed the assignment. Why kill him and not question him? Damn! He'd been played for a fool.

Michelle saw his highly-strung machismo ebb away. She'd hit a nerve. The light had been turned on in his head.

'Don't you see? You have been working for him all this time! He knows who you are and now we know your motives we can deal with you in the matter to which you have grown accustomed.'

The unknown man was suddenly beginning to feel very small. He knew he couldn't trust anyone, but his superior? Surely not. Maybe he had been allowed to get rid of GEMINI and The Boss as a way to highlight his own existence. If it was true, then they had been watching him for months and they knew his every move. He had to get out of here but his body was stiff, stunned by the revelation.

'I think we're done here,' said Michelle as she knocked back the last couple of swigs of her wine. She gathered her things, leaving a ten-pound note resting on her placemat to pay for her drink. As she went to get up she looked at her companion. His mind was lost in a sea of thought. The plan had worked.

'Don't follow me, I really don't recommend it,' whispered Michelle into his ear as she walked the few metres to the door, which enveloped onto the dark street of the city.

The unknown man shook his thoughts from his head and turned around to see the girl leaving the café. He sprung out of his seat and went to pursue her through the night. As he walked through the sporadic crowd of people he kept her in his eye line, walking at a pace just a couple of metres away.

All the while his head was swimming with the thoughts of doubt that this strong girl had put in his head. Had she been lying? Surely the Big Chief didn't know who he was? If he did then there was only one person he could be. This was serious.

The unknown man's life, indeed the mystery he had sworn to keep surrounding himself, was in danger. First though, he had to stop Michelle.

*

As she walked down the street, Michelle knew that she was being followed. She laughed to herself.

Bless him; he just doesn't know when to give up. She slowed her pace down, allowing her pursuer to catch up with her.

There was one surprise that she had left up her sleeve. To her right, there was an alley that she could lure him down.

The unknown man gained a few feet on his prey. He noticed her wheel down an alleyway.

Typical. She must have a gang of goons down there just ready to pounce on him. He tensed his body and prepared himself for a fistfight. He had just entered the alley when...

WHACK!

Pain shot across the back of his head. The unknown man fell to the floor, his eyesight blurring at the same time as a cracking headache began to blanket his judgment.

Fighting the comfort of unconsciousness, he staggered to try and regain his balance, only to be met by another crack on his cranium. This time it was a foot, which forced itself into his face. He could feel the pain burn his nose – maybe, he thought, it was broken.

As blood began to seep from a fresh wound in his forehead and his body fell heavily to the floor, he could just make out the figure of a woman in front of him, then he fell face down in the muddy alley, unable to stay conscious.

Michelle breathed a sigh of relief. 'Told you,' she quipped as she put the knuckle-duster back in her handbag, allowing herself to smile smugly at the fact that she had just beaten up one of the most dangerous men in the city. The Big Chief would be proud.

Those self-defence classes he made her attend had come in very handy. She left the unknown man in the alley, walking towards a car that was conveniently parked about ten yards down the road. Inside there were two people. A driver and a passenger.

She opted for the back seat and got in, the features of her accomplices obscured by the blacked-out windows. No words were exchanged as she clambered into the car and the vehicle started up and drove off into the night.

A few hours later, the unknown man awoke with a searing headache and a bump on the back and front of his head. The wound that was just above his left eye had solidified and gingerly he picked himself up off the dirty alley.

He caressed the bump on the back of his head as his eyesight returned to sharp focus. *The girl? It couldn't have been.* If it was, he thought to himself, he couldn't tell his superior about this. The embarrassment would be excruciating. His superior! Suddenly he remembered what Michelle had told him. He needed to get to a phone and quick.

After tonight, nothing and nobody could be trusted. He had to know, he had to make sure. Had he been dancing with the devil all this time? The unknown man straightened himself up and lurched out of the alley onto the street. This had gone far enough.

CHAPTER FOUR

FATE DEAL

The scrape of dry branches swished across the unknown man's body as he hurtled through the wood. Sweat dripping down his face, and the sunshine piercing the trees above him; he could feel the hot stinging pain throb in his rib cage and the blood seep through the open wound in his left leg.

He was limping, but even with an injury he was still fast enough to keep his hunters at bay.   With a flashing glance he could make out the outlines of three bodies pursuing him, undeterred by the trouble the unknown man had caused them in the past hour and spurred on by the fight he had put up. It wasn't the men who were the main problem he thought. He could get away from them.

Oh sure, the injuries he had sustained were enough to stop any normal man, but the unknown man was not a normal person. He had taught himself to manipulate pain and turn it into a positive − something which he could block out and harness as a target to fix as soon as he was out of his predicament. The real problem for him was the dogs that they had released off their leashes that were gaining on him.

Over the sounds of his own breath becoming heavier he could hear the snarling jaws of the hounds drawing nearer. His own pace had dropped a little and the uneven ground in the wood made for even more agony on his wounded leg.

The unknown man gritted his teeth as the concentration on harnessing his uncomfortable state began to slip under the stress of this new distraction.

On he went, his sprint became a limp; the red-hot touch of pain drawing him ever nearer to a full stop. The woods were beginning to thin out as he dragged his battling body through the last few feet of trees.

The barking was closer than it had been before and the unknown man's resilience had finally given way. After nearly two miles, the chase was over.

As he fell to the floor, crying out in agony, the unknown man resisted caressing his wounds.

Doing that would only make the pain worse and force him to give in. Instead, he looked up, desperately looking for something that would help him out of his situation.

His vision hazy, he scanned his surroundings yet never forgot the sound of the dogs that were approaching him.

There was a little shack, which was about half a mile to his right and just hidden away from the clearing.

Thank God, he thought.

He knew that if he could just shoulder the agony for a little while longer he could reach it.

But first, he had to deal with his latest friends.

He turned onto his back, facing the wolf-like dogs that were nearly on top of him. They were less than ten seconds away. He checked that he still had his gun in his tattered jacket pocket.

Seven seconds.

He snapped the gun back and saw that he had only one bullet remaining. Four seconds. He looked up.

Two dogs, drooling and barking at their fallen meal.

One might be enough, thought the unknown man. The canine duo sprang up through the air and descended on their bleeding prey.

BANG!

The first hound fell to the ground, yelping and stricken by the bullet, which had penetrated its body. The other pounced on the unknown man and sunk its slobbery teeth into his arm.

Screaming in agony, the unknown man leapt to his feet and the dog's weight began to pull down on where it had bitten him. There it dangled, gnawing at his limb as he desperately tried to shake it off.

Its teeth puncturing his skin and muscle, the hound snarled at its victim, staring into his tortured eyes. The agony was blinding him.

Then, as if from nowhere, all of the strength left in his battered, bleeding body mustered the dog in the air and with a mighty swoop, the unknown man swatted the mutt through the air and into a nearby tree, knocking it unconscious.

The Dog's teeth had ripped a mighty chunk out of his flesh and then his teeth dragged like a rake along the skin as the hound vacated the limb.

The unknown man staggered out into the clearing, holding his bleeding frame up as best as he could.

He looked back: the dog he had shot was only wounded and still alive and the other lay prostrate on the leaf-strewn dirt.

Crimson droplets began to seep quicker out of his leg and arm but still, he carried on, pushing his tortured body ever closer to the shack. The men who were pursuing him had obviously stopped for breath, thinking that their dogs would have him.

Stupid fools, thought the unknown man, although he knew they would catch up sooner or later. He'd have to rest, and with no cars in sight in the rural location, the shack was the only option.

He stumbled to the ground again just a few metres away from his destination. Forgoing the temptation to inspect his injuries he crawled, with all the effort of a man up a cliff face, to the little forgotten shack.

A voice in his head questioned if the door was locked or not. He couldn't shoot his way in with no more ammunition! Luckily, the lock on the latch was hanging off, so the unknown man was able, with all his strength, to haul his broken self into safety.

Shutting the door with his injury-free right leg, he whimpered as he lay on the muddy floor.

After closing his eyes and regaining his breath for a few moments, he glanced down at his arm. Removing the tatters of what had been the arm of his jacket he stared in horror at the bloody mess that his right arm was now in.

He screamed at the sight, betraying his manly mannerisms.

Regaining his senses, he then covered it up, stopping the flow of blood with what remained of his jacket.

With his good arm, he pulled his left leg up and inspected the blood-soaked material of his trouser. His ribs ached as he twisted his body but after the grizzly inspection, he came to the conclusion that the worst part of his injuries was the dog bite.

'Bastards!' he cursed loudly. 'They will pay for this!'

Lying back, and allowing himself a few minutes of relaxation, the unknown man began to retrace the last couple of hours. How could he have let this happen? How on earth was he caught out so badly? He had been played for a fool for such a long time; the deal he had made with his superior back then was haunting him now.

Closing his eyes and giving in to the bliss of unconsciousness, these events and the mystery of the Big Chief played out in his head and he remembered his fateful meeting just two hours ago....

*

The sky beamed down a beautiful blue on the unknown man as he sped his Porsche convertible along the country roads. The cool spring wind flowed through the car as it twisted its way through the rural landscape.

Fields where the yellowish crops were budding in their soft beds enveloped the unknown man, who was unstirred as the natural beauty he was travelling through surrounded the little silver car.

He was finally going to get the answers he had been looking for.

It had been the longest week of his life. After his humiliating meeting with Michelle, which had only bruised his ego and determination, the unknown man had been left embarrassed at the uncertainty of his part in the bigger picture.

He knew in his head that his superior had assigned him to kill The Boss and wipe out the leaders of GEMINI in what he thought was a routine job.

In his cold heart, he knew that there was a massive possibility that his superior was acting under the Big Chief: apparently the master of the puppets in this once noble, clean country.

The Big Chief stalked the unknown man's thoughts throughout his every waking moment. He hated the scum that tore out the heart of the country he lived in and even in his dishonest line of work; he liked to think he made a contribution to the destruction of hard crime.

Christ, maybe I should have become a policeman! He thought to himself. He smiled and shook his head. Of course not, he was far too honest for that job.

After another twenty minutes on the same road, the car turned to its right and the sight of the rendezvous spot came into the unknown man's peripheral vision. 'Jesus, he sure knows how to pick them,' he muttered to himself, gazing through his reflective sunglasses onto the open gates, which led to a disused recycling plant.

It looked like the owners had vacated not so long ago and the scene was a bleak one compared to what the unknown man had driven through.

Still, his mind was on the meeting with his superior, and what he was going to say. He wasn't going to hold back.

Before he pulled up in the car park, he checked his insurance – a fully loaded handgun in the top of his jacket pocket. He didn't want to use it, but if he had to, then he'd need it where it was easily obtainable.

He looked around the car park. A white van was parked adjacent to him and two sleek-looking Mercedes were parked opposite. The car of crooks thought the unknown man as he left his vehicle and proceeded to the meeting place – behind the plant, next to the heaps of rubbish. '*Suspicious*' was not the word that was buzzing in his mind. '*Set-up*' was.

Still, he had to be stout and pretend that he knew less than he did. His superior wasn't going to get the better of him if he was under the control of the Big Chief.

68

The unknown man looked around him and took in the mounds of disregarded rubbish. He thought it odd that nobody was working on site.

The sound of approaching feet marching towards him disrupted his thoughts. As he turned around, four men dressed in smart dinner jackets and trousers approached him. Leading the advance was an elderly man, with grey hair and a friendly face that was beaming as he walked towards the unknown man, with an outstretched hand greeting him.

'There you are,' said the old man, who out stretched a hand for the unknown man to shake. He examined it thoroughly and then shook it with a strong grip. He looked into the old man's hazel eyes. He was about sixty, well built yet not overweight and his face was deeply lined. The unknown man's superior looked admiringly at his protégé.

'How was the trip?' he said, relinquishing their handshake.

'Fine, nice to get out of the city once in a while,' replied the unknown man, who looked around him again, 'But you could have chosen a setting which was easier on the eye.'

'Come now, we're not in the property market now are we? Besides, it's a Sunday, nobody works here today, it's a good thing I'm not one for praying otherwise I'd have some explaining to do with the man upstairs for missing communion.'

69

The superior went for his pocket and produced a pack of cigarettes; he lit one before offering the rest of the pack to the unknown man, who declined with a shake of the head.

'Right,' said the superior between puffs, 'Now what is this about?'

'Sir, since that job on The Boss in February I have made some enquiries into this so-called Big Chief that everyone seems to be scared of.'

The Superior raised an eyebrow: 'Oh, have you now?' His soft face-hardened a little, as if a sheet of metal had filmed over his features.

'Yes, sir,' continued the unknown man. 'At first I thought that the job on The Boss was just a routine one, something you wanted me to handle. The man was filth and we got him off the streets, but then sometime after I found out about his involvement with GEMINI.'

'Yes I know,' said the superior 'Shame you didn't take any prisoners son, we could have done with more information.'

This surprised the unknown man. Wasn't his job to make sure that GEMINI ceased to be, whatever the cost?

'Anyway, through one of GEMINI's agents I met a girl called Michelle Simmons, she's a personal assistant to Sir Michael Houghton, and we all know who he is in charge of.'

'The police, what's that got to do with it?'

70

'Sir, she led me to believe that the Big Chief doesn't just control the city. He controls the whole country! He has got every dirty finger in every dirty pie and controls everything.'

'And you listened to her?'

'It was all beginning to add up. The criminal figureheads were going unpunished for years until they fell afoul of the big man himself, when they were easily punished and eventually killed after they were made to suffer. But it isn't just the criminals, sir; can't you see that we are all being used? We have been assassinating these gang lords and doing the Big Chief's dirty work!'

'Rubbish,' replied the superior. 'The reason that I told you to dispose of The Boss was because of the danger their alliance would have brought to the city. It is not our area to probe into other shenanigans. Well, not yet anyway. I assign you your work in accordance with the threat and not because we are controlled by a mightier power. Christ, I've been a part of the Secret Service for forty years man and boy! Do you not think that I would have sensed something amiss, even back then, and stopped it?'

The old man sighed and regained his composure. His young counterpart had to be reassured.

'You are my best man. I can rely on you. That is why you carry out the jobs that must not be interfered with. Do you remember when you joined us?'

The unknown man was reminded of different days. Everything seemed to be brighter in his minds-eye back then, before the splash of blood and pain had closed his heart to everything that could and had hurt him.

'You were so young, naïve too, but a talent none the less,' continued the old man. 'I knew that given the right training and guidance you would become my most prized asset and maybe my most trusted employee. We made a deal which ultimately decided your destiny. It was a fate deal that has developed you into one of us. Something, which has set you above those who you kill, changed you and for that, you became stronger, less vulnerable. Of course the sacrifices you made to get here must not have been easy, but nonetheless, you are the jewel in our crown.'

He looked at the unknown man, who felt as if someone had unlocked a door to the past. He remembered those he left behind, who he could not bear to see in danger. Then he remembered Rachel and his cold heart sank.

'You are my number one, so trust me when I say this. We are out in the open, alone. There is no higher power, no sugar

72

daddy financing us. Our side of the service is exclusive and safe from the Big Chief and his web.'

'You speak as though we aren't looking for a fight with this person: what's protecting us?'

'Our history,' replied the unknown man's superior. 'If the Big Chief tries to take us down then we'll take him down with us. Because we have got the best of the best and he knows that.'

'And who is that?' enquired the unknown man.

'You,' smiled his superior. 'Now, let's stop this suspicion and go grab some food. I know a lovely little cottage that has been converted into a pub and my appetite craves a roast dinner,' he put his hand on his protégé's shoulder and led him back towards the car park.

The unknown man had been suspicious of the four men who had observed their conversation back on the rubbish heap. He had noticed that while his superior was talking about the Big Chief, one of the men had twitched slightly. Maybe it was his suspicion but still, something was not right.

'I must ask, what's with all the extra protection?' he asked.

'Never mind.'

'Sir, has the Big Chief threatened you?'

'No, not at all but...it's always a good idea to keep yourself protected.'

The unknown man gulped, 'Oh?'

'Well, you have taken apart the info structure of the Big Chief's plans. I can't have my best man wasted in a revenge attack now can I? No no, I was going to leave it for the car journey but   I suppose I'd better tell you now. The Big Chief has ordered a bounty on your head. After your recent adventures it seems he wants you dead more than the rest of his enemies. We think it is because in the grander scheme of things, GEMINI's deal with The Boss was part of a bigger picture, one we are still trying to piece together.'

'I can understand the gesture but I do not need protection.'

'Nonsense. It's only a precautionary measure. Why do you think I had to get you out of the city and out here? The Big Chief won't try to find you out here. The pub I am taking you to, after our meal I want you to stay there for a few days. Let us deal with what the Big Chief has got planned. Let the heat die down a bit'.

The unknown man resented this gesture. He didn't like to be wrapped up in cotton wool.

This didn't feel like a welcome break to him. It felt like a punishment.

Quietly, and out of the respect of his superior, he accepted it. Now it was time for the burning question.

'So, do we know who the Big Chief is?'

'Unfortunately not. There have been many possibilities over the years but none have been exposed as the genuine article. Look, don't worry. Leave everything up to us.'

One of the heavies approached the two men. 'If you would like to step this way sir, we shall take you on ahead,' he looked at the unknown man.

'Maybe you could follow us to the pub?'

'Of course,' said the unknown man. 'I'll see you in a bit, how far away is this place?'

'Not long, about ten minutes,' said the heavy. 'We shall see you there.'

As the two agents shook hands and walked to their respective cars, deep down the unknown man was extremely cautious of his superior's guards.

He opened the driver's door to his Porsche and looked in the wing mirror at the car that his boss was departing in. At the same time, three of the men approached the white van and clambered inside.

'This isn't right,' the unknown man muttered to himself.

He glanced back in his wing mirror just in time to witness his superior enter his car and drive off past him, prompting the unknown man to start the Porsche up and proceed out of the gates after them.

The white van started up and followed suit.

75

The men in the car grinned with glee. They had him.

After five minutes the windy roads died down into straight narrow lanes. The unknown man, who was doing forty in his convertible, heard the roar of a diesel engine behind him. It was the white van.

He watched as they gained speed on his rather impressive motor. His eyes diverted back to the road in front of him when he felt a hard thump from behind. The car jolted and he turned his head.

The van was trying to ram him.

He shouted at the driver and sped his car up again, now only a few feet from the rear of his superior's car. The Porsche jolted again, this time the shatter of glass on his taillight followed the thud. He knew it.

Spies.

A couple more thuds later and the Porsche was in danger of colliding with the Mercedes in front. Had his superior noticed what was going on?

Apparently not.

The unknown man wrestled with his steering wheel to regain some control. The narrow roads and constricting space was causing him all sorts of problems. He had to lure the spies away from his boss.

After several more shunts from the white van, the Porsche swung off the straight road and into another winding lane. The white van, ignoring the superior's Mercedes, gave chase and accelerated hard to catch the sports car.

As the unknown man sped down the country back roads he hoped that there were no other cars on the road. Casualties were the last thing he wanted, apart from those who were chasing him.

Spies working for the Big Chief himself, he thought. This wasn't the first time that people had wanted him dead, but he was going to make sure that it was the last.

As the clash of metal on metal grinded through the countryside, inside the white van, the heavies had their prey just where they wanted him. They had waited for a long time to dispose of the unknown man, months of working inside the firm, watching his every move from within the system.

The moles had infiltrated the so-called impregnable palace, the last company that wasn't under their master's control. It had taken them years to get there, but now the firm would be at their mercy. Now they were so close to overcoming the final hurdle.

The white van continued to crash its way along the narrow road and into the now battered sports car.

As the unknown man continued to wrestle with his vehicle he just survived a passing car, which honked in anger at the warring motors.

The roads became windier still, one final clunk from the white van proved fatal to the Porsche.

In a blur of silver, the convertible took off, the control relinquished and the unknown man braced himself for impact.

The next few seconds were painful and went by faster than the speed of light. The white van decreased speed to watch the Porsche flip into a trench at the side of the road and bed itself upside down on a field.

Driving by the crash site, they pulled up in a lay-by ten metres further ahead. Two of the men got out of the vehicle, while the other was more preoccupied by something in the back behind the grating between the boot and the cockpit.

The heavies smiled sinisterly as their eyes gazed at the carnage in front of them. The crippled Porsche was smoking, broken beyond repair.

What of the man inside?

The unknown man lay dazed on the earth, his seatbelt broken in the impact. His body obscured by the overturned car, he assessed his injuries. His ribs ached, possibly broken from impact with the steering wheel as the car flipped. What hurt more was a gash in his left leg, the cause too hard to tell in the darkness.

Although uncomfortable, the unknown man was lucky to have survived with the injuries he had obtained.

Now came the hard bit. He could hear the sound of footsteps approaching his destroyed car. Time to play dead.

The heavies readied their guns and then they pulled their prisoner out of the wreck by his jacket. The victim was unconscious, but he was still alive. Time to finish him off once and for all. As the men cocked they're guns, they levelled them at his head.

'Take this you son of a bit -'

The heavy didn't finish his statement, and found himself falling back onto the ground. With a precision swing of his good leg, the unknown man had connected with the goon's torso and knocked the wind out of his sails.

With his eyes now open, he kicked the gun out of the other man's hand before he had a chance to fire.

Leaping to his feet, and then shrieking at the pain in his chest, the unknown man grabbed the second man and forced his head down onto the undercarriage of his car wreck.

The heavy screamed in pain and fell to the floor, blood beginning to pour from his nose. The first heavy had leapt to his feet and shot at the unknown man, who felt the bullet whistle past his arm and into the Porsche. He withdrew his own gun and fired.

Missed.

His eyes were blurry from the shock of the crash and it became even worse when the first heavy threw him into the twisted metal. One blow to the face and then another to his ribcage made the unknown man's body flood with the hot gush of pain.

He recoiled but, using the car to steady himself, he swung at his enemy and caught him a glancing blow on the jaw.

As the heavy fell to the floor, the unknown man went to pick his gun up and finish them off.

However, since the spies were also working for the same firm they had been issued with the same gun and he had picked up one of the heavies firearms.

Not knowing this he readied to fire on his main tormentor: the first heavy who had been at the wheel of the white van. But before he did the second thug, bellowing instructions to the van, interrupted him.

'Get the dogs!'

Face flushing to white, the unknown man's pupils dilated. Even with a fully loaded gun, he did not know how many dogs there were. All of a sudden his predicament grew instantly more challenging.

He looked at the two men on the floor, slowly regaining their strength.

He looked on at the white van, which a third man had jumped out of, who was opening the doors at the rear to the sound of panting and snarling.

He had to run for it. It was his only chance.

Testing his bad leg, he stuttered into a limp and gradually paced into a fast sprint towards woodland deep in the field.

The two stricken heavies were by now back on their feet and once joined by their colleague with the two hounds −straining at their leashes to strip flesh – they set off after him.

Whatever happened next, they couldn't fail. Otherwise, their lives wouldn't be worth living.   The wounded party recommenced their hunt as up ahead, the unknown man, concentrating on not surrendering to the pain of his injuries, entered the wood.

And now here he was, not long after, lying semi-conscious on the floor of a shack. A once powerful, almost indestructible mysterious entity, bleeding and broken on the muddy floor. Eyes closed, the replaying of his recent memories ceased when he was disturbed by the sound of somebody trying to get into the shack.   Had they found him already? If they had, this was truly the end. He was in no shape to continue the battle. He hated to admit it to himself but this looked like the end.

Still mentally shaken by his ordeal, the unknown man gazed up at the shadowed figure through the small glass window in the door.

Now almost too weak to move, he reached for a nearby spade and in a futile attempt to raise it above his head groaned in agony.

At that moment, the figure, as the sunlight irradiated around their silhouette, forced the stiff door open and gazed down on the bloody stranger on the floor…

CHAPTER FIVE

BATTERY FOR THE BONES

'What the…what the bloody hell are you doing in here?'

Jill Adams stared in disbelief at the wounded stranger who lay bleeding on the floor of her shack.

She had only entered the little wooden hut to begin a long overdue clear out of its contents and what better day, she thought, than a Sunday when the sun glistens through the blue sky.

It was the kind of weather that was needed after her recent bereavement and it helped her muster the strength of will to finally dispose of the things her dearly departed had used for so many years.

She had been plagued with a silly fear of rats since she was a little girl, betraying her usual stiff upper lip manner that she had adopted from her father when she was young.

Jill had dreaded coming across them in the lonely hut and prepared to meet her fear head on. What she hadn't prepared for, was a different sort of lodger all together.

The stranger could barely keep his eyes open.

The spade, which he had clasped in his good arm, fell to the ground when his strength gave way. It clanged on the ground making Jill jump.

'Please,' he gasped, 'help me.'

She surveyed his frame. There was a nasty gash in his left leg. His arm looked like it had been set upon by a big animal and his face was covered in sweat and crimson dots. Before Jill could reply the stranger fainted.

Her eyes wide with shock, she leant down and immediately went about making her wounded patient comfortable. Even if this man was a violent person, or a criminal, he was in no fit state to pose Jill any harm. Spotting a bag of compost, she dragged it across the floor and used it as a pillow for the stranger.

Improvising, she used the torn part of the man's jacket sleeve as a bandage on his gashed leg. Then the dreaded part came.

Taking a deep breath, she pulled back the tatters of cloth that had been the man's jacket arm and gazed at the damaged arm. Jill recoiled, choking back the feeling of nausea that had suddenly overcome her. She gagged, but then pulled herself together and tightened the wound with the clothing and held it up in the air.

At that moment, the man stirred back into consciousness,

possibly because the pain was so intense in this part of his body. With his good arm, he grabbed her and pulled her forward.

'Don - don't let them...find me.'

She squealed, and then as the man fell back into a deep sleep, she sighed deeply. Was he on the run, she thought? She couldn't just leave him there, even if he was possibly dragging her into danger with him.

No, he'd have to come back with him.

Gathering her senses, and her strength, she decided to pull the man up by his least damaged side of his body.

Good god he was heavy! she thought.

'Look, if you want my help sonny you'll have to be a bit more co-operative, come on, my Landy is outside.'

With a struggle, Jill dragged the wounded party to her Land Rover, which was only a matter of feet away. Propping him up against the vehicle, she made sure the padlock was firmly in place on the shack door so it didn't arouse suspicion. Luckily, no blood was spilt on the door, but she still wiped her smeared hands on her coat and went back to her patient, picking him up again.   Looking about her, and buckling under the stranger's weight, she couldn't see anybody else in the field. All of a sudden, she heard distant cries from within the woods, about half a mile away. These must have been the

85

people this person was hiding from.

She redoubled her efforts, opened the back door to her vehicle and carefully slumped the stranger in the back.

Tucking his legs in, she closed the metal door behind him and ran to the driver's door. Diving in and now feeling the pressure of a possible encounter with the monsters that had done this to that poor man, she pleaded with the engine to start.

It gave nothing, not even a wimper of life.

Old Land Rovers occasionally did this, yet when it finally coughed into life, the din could be heard for miles around. It was so loud, the unknown man stirred again in the back. 'Drive!' he curdled, just as the tyres screeched and the old vehicle sped down the dirt track and away from the shack.

*

The unknown man awoke from a feverish dream lying in a bed. He was startled by his surroundings. He lay in a single bed, in what looked like a bedroom in a cottage. The wooden beams were a dead giveaway to the room's age, *17th century*, he thought.

The football paraphernalia that adorned the walls though meant that the room must belong to a youngster.

Bolt upright, the unknown man finished surveying his

location and looked at his injuries. His leg felt much better, whatever had caused the gash must have only caused a slight flesh wound.

It was bound and the pain he had felt in the forest had melted into an ache. His ribs were sore, and when he inhaled sharply a pain shot through his chest.

He fell back onto the soft, welcoming pillows. Wincing for a while, he regained his senses and dared to look at his arm. It was fixed in a crude sling that was tied behind his neck. With his healthy arm, he probed the contents of the sling.

He hissed through his pain as his fingers felt the damaged tissue. He was interrupted by the bedroom door opening, which made him jump in his crumpled sheets.

'Sorry to startle you,' said Jill, She had prepared a tea tray of tea and biscuits for the stranger. 'Here, I made you a drink in case you were awake this time. Your last one looks stone cold and barely touched. You must have been shattered with all those injuries.'

The unknown man watched her as she replenished the cup on the side mantle.

'Thank you Miss err?'

'MRS Adams,' she corrected him. 'That's okay; well I couldn't just leave you there all beaten and bruised. I had wanted to call for an ambulance but in your feverish state you told me not to…oh careful with the tea the bed has just been changed. Sit up straight.'

The unknown man was in no mood to be bossed about but since this lady had taken him in and tended to his wounds he was just grateful to be safe.

'Now you're awake, can I ask you some questions?

'I thought you'd say that.'

Jill found this retort a little rude.

'Well what do you expect? I take a stranger in who I find trespassing in my shed who looks like he's had a battering from Ali, tend to him, clothe him and let him stay in my house.'

'Okay, I'm sorry; of course you can ask me anything.'

'Thank you. Who are you and what were you doing in the woods?'

'I was out walking in the fields when a stray pit bull attacked me. I tried to get away and I eventually did when I found your shack.'

'Interesting' she pondered, pulling his gun out of her jacket.

'Then why did you have this on you then, eh?' 'Found it,' he replied. 'And you say those injuries were given to you by a dog? Sorry I don't believe you. I'm a mother of two sons so don't think that I can't detect when a young man is lying to me.'

'You're a clever woman,' said the unknown man.

'And you shouldn't insult my intelligence,' Jill said. 'So whatever trouble you are in, don't bring it to my door. I'm not well equipped to fight off an army of thugs.'

'Look, I am incredibly grateful. I won't give you any trouble and neither will anybody else.' He began to make an effort to get out of bed. 'I can't let you go in this state, and if you are refusing hospital treatment then I really don't know what to do.'

'I don't want to be any trouble. I'm sure I will be able to make it back to my…car.'

The unknown man paused for a moment, remembering the state of his beloved Porsche and the Big Chief's spies who had run him off the road and attacked him.

And what of his superior? Had he been in on the act? He had lured him out here to the supposed safety of the countryside while the firm investigated the Big Chief's empire, but it all could have been a trap, to get him away, to kill him and dispose of his being and let the kingpin take over his employers too. One thing was inevitable.

The company was rife with bugs. His mind began to race through the evidence for and against his superior's betrayal when Jill interrupted.

'You're not from around here are you?'

'Err no; I came out here for a short holiday, to get away from my busy life back in the city.'

'I see, do you have anywhere to stay?'

'Not necessarily, my boss had planned for me to stay at a local pub, but I forget the name.'

'Well it can't be The Crown, that place went ages ago. You see there's no money out in the country anymore. That's what Henry used t...I mean that's what he says. No, your boss must have meant the Red Lion. But in your state it looks like you'll just have to stay here for a while, stay where you are and I'll just have to take you on face value.'

'You're very kind; I'll give you some money for your troubles.'

'That's alright, now what do I call you?'

The unknown man hesitated. *Time to get creative.*

'Call me David.'

'Nice to meet you David. My name is Jill,' she smiled. 'Do your children still live here? I can't think they will be best pleased that a stranger is lying in one of their beds.'

'Oh no, they moved out years ago. One is an estate agent in Bournemouth. The other, my youngest whose room you are in is a Journalist. All of these old posters are from his favourite team, Tottenham Hotspur. Do you like football?'

'Yes, they are my team too, haven't been to the Lane for

years now though. The last time I went Danny Blanchflower
was the captain and Jimmy Greaves was the best player. Well,
that's what people said anyway. I always rather admired Dave
Mackay, myself.'

The unknown man began to look back through rose tinted
glasses at his days on the terraces, watching the lilywhites on
that field of dreams known by everyone as White Hart Lane.

'He and his father used to go when he was little.' Jill started
taking the clothes off the radiator that was situated under the
window.

'I take it that your husband at home today?'   Jill turned
her back to 'David' and looked longingly out of the window.

'He is…away, farmer's fair. Won't be back for a couple of
days. He wanted me to clear out the shed in his absence.
Looks like I'll have to do it another day now. Anyway you just
lie there and get better, I'll make you some food if you want,
and you must be starving, lying there for two days.'

'Two days! Is that how long I have been out?' Jill nodded.

'I didn't want to wake you; you were in a terrible state. I had
wanted to get a doctor in to look at that dog bite but after
cleaning it up I don't think that it was so bad. A few stitches
sufficed with the gash and your arm. It's a good thing you
happened to break in to the shed of a nurse!'

'Yes, about time I had some luck,' said the unknown man.

91

He put his cup of tea down and breathed deeply. His ribs had softened in the pain he was experiencing. He pondered on the events that had lead to his current situation. One man had driven off his superior while the other three left in the white van and attacked him. Was his superior kidnapped too? If that were the case, then the common enemy would have completed his jigsaw with the final piece. That, and his current fitness, was all he could think about. Then a question popped up in his head.

'So your husband's been away for four days and left you to clear out an old shed?'

Jill sighed. 'Yes…pity, you could have had somebody else to talk to besides a middle aged woman, you and him could have reminisced about football for hours on end.' The unknown man looked at her. She was a widow. Jill was obviously not over the recent death of her beloved husband and his appearance had interrupted her bereavement.

He had interrupted her attempts to clear out his old shed and she still changed her son's beds because it harked back to her old routine.

Poor woman.

She seemed nice and probably could do with some company for a while.

He decided to rest there for a bit like she said, with all the information still configuring in his head, he could not be sure that the offer back to the pub would have been as much of a trap as the meeting at the recycling plant. He detested some part of his job.

The ambiguity, the blood on his hands and the mystery of the night, which played out as a backdrop to his killer instincts.

He could never trust anyone.

That's why he had never revealed his name to anybody in his business. That was why he had even gone to the trouble of striking it from his permanent records. Sometimes, he thought to himself, that if he stayed in this god-awful profession for much longer, he would forget it forever.

It was one of the few precious things he had left and he didn't want it spoiled by the bloodshed he was responsible for. If only Jill knew what he did for a living she would reach for the phone and dial 999 quicker than he could move.

'So, what line of work are you in?' Jill said.

'Oh, it's not that interesting really.'

'Go on.'

'I'm an estate agent. I work for a private firm called Southgates and I've worked there for twelve years.'

'So you didn't go to university then?' Jill enquired.

'What makes you say that?'

'Well judging by your age, did you go straight from school?

93

'I'm not as young as I look,' the unknown man cracked a smile, the first he had mustered in a very long time. 'But I'm flattered by the remark.'

'That's alright,' Jill replied, playing with the pile of clothes she had taken off the radiator.

'Anyway I'd best get on with this lot, let me know if there was anything you wanted.' 'Would it be okay if I could use your phone? I'd better let the office know what has happened.'

'Of course, hold on I'll go and get it, just relax, you'll be up on your feet in no time.' Jill smiled and then left the room.

'You're very kind,' the unknown man felt humbled, but knew that he had to speak to his superior. He decided to let him know he was alive, but not his location. Just in case he was part of the trap.

Jill returned with the phone, which she placed on the bedside table. She picked up the empty cup that the unknown man had finished. The unknown man smiled at Jill as she left the room and lifted the receiver up to his ear, dialling his firm's number as his temporary landlady closed the bedroom door behind her. She paused outside, and then decided not to listen in on the conversation. The unknown man heard her footsteps ebb away from the door and then began speaking.

'It's me…get him,' he whispered, his voice returning to its

more serious tone, which had slipped when in the presence of Jill.

He waited patiently for half a minute and heard the mumble of his superior as he neared the other receiver.

'What the hell happened to you?' he barked.

'I had a little trouble with the friends you brought along to our meeting.'

'They didn't report back either, what on earth happened? I waited at the pub for three hours before we sent a search party out. After we found your car we thought you had been done for. By the way I don't think it will pass its next MOT,' he joked.

'NO, sir,' the unknown man was in no mood for humour. 'I was attacked. The three men in the white van. They are working for the Big Chief. This is important sir; there are bugs inside our system.'

'Good lord', replied his superior, 'we'd best get the pest control in, sounds like we have bugs. Where are you now?'

'I'm safe, I don't know my location but they got to me. I'm a bit bruised but I should be okay in a few days.'

'That is just the news I wanted to hear,' the old man's voice twinkled with this turn of optimism. 'Our men have been looking into the situation with the Big Chief. You were right. A member of Sir Michael Houghton's staff is a spy in the employ of the Big Chief.'

'Michelle! I knew it!' the unknown man's memories rewound to his encounter with the femme fatale. It must be her. She knew too much at the time.

'We're tracking her as we speak. You just get better and report back here when you're fully recovered. Don't worry. We're on the case. We don't anticipate the pieces moving on the board too much until your return,' the old man's authority shone through the receiver and the unknown man sat bolted upright as if he were right in front of him.

'Do we have a name sir, is it definitely Michelle?'

'We do. Black Diamond. It may not be her, but she is the only lead we have until then. We'll start clearing the office of bugs and hopefully by the time we see you next they will be gone and we'll have some more information. Remember, the name we have got is Black Diamond. A codename for sure. We have to accept all possibilities that this person could turn out to be Sir Michael himself so recharge yourself and get some rest, relax and get back here as soon as you can run without breaking into a sweat.'

'I will sir, a good rest is what is needed, thank you, we'll have our pub lunch some other day.'

'I'll hold you to it. Okay son, take it easy. Call us before you arrive.'

The line went dead. The unknown man's trust for his superior was regained within the short but direct phone call. The firm had actively gone on his information and a corner piece of the Big Chief's puzzle had been found out. The Big Chief had made his first big mistake.

He was still alive and they were edging closer to the big man himself.

The unknown man slumped back into his sheets and thought quietly to himself.

The game was back on.

CHAPTER SIX

BLACK DIAMOND

The small yet elegant house had played out many important meetings in the past. Soon to be monarchs and Prime Ministers have debated endlessly for hours upon hours within the Georgian building. Its position in the heart of Mayfair made for one of the prettier housing estates in the city, the white bricks looming with authority over passers-by.

Outside, a well-dressed man in a top hat stood to attention. His buttons and shoes polished, his three-piece suit immaculately ironed: guaranteeing no creases.

His face, lined from old age, felt cold in the breeze. Spring had been a cold one this year, he thought to himself.

He had been waiting for the black cab for around five minutes and he knew nothing of what the members of parliament were going to discuss. It wasn't his place to ask; he knew only to obey, but how he would love to have been a fly on the wall sometimes.

As he pondered the possibilities of the topics to himself, a black cab, followed by a police car, came into view out of the corner of his eye. He stood with his head held high and walked down the steps leading to the front door to where the black cab was parking.

Leaning down to open the rear passenger door, he could see two men sitting opposite one another in the vehicle. Opening the door, a tall man in his late fifties, with greying hair and a serious look on his face, departed the cab first.

A second man, also in his fifties, followed him – but his hair was still sandy blonde. He had no need to hunch down to leave the vehicle since he was considerably smaller than his counterpart, if not a little more rotund. Stepping on to the kerb, he stood alongside his colleague and waited for the doorman to show them inside.

Patiently, they followed the doorman up the stairs after he closed the cab door and entered the old house in a line. Whilst inside, they politely took off their long coats and handed them to the doorman, who carefully placed them on the hat stand. 'Shall we?' said the grey haired man, holding out an arm to direct his colleague into the main living quarters.

The second man smiled at the gesture and they both proceeded to the posh surroundings. The doorman leaned forward to close the door for the two men, but following a glare from the taller man, he stood up straight and walked away.

Before shutting the door behind him, he maintained his stare and closed the door slowly once the doorman was out of sight.

'Well I must say Sir Michael; it really is a beautiful house. You should be proud of it you know, you've come a long way since we first met.' The second man had made himself at home and was sitting on one of the lush, auburn sofas that were at his disposal.

'Being a member of parliament rewards you with such privileges,' said Sir Michael, who brushed his grey hair back with his left hand and walked towards another sofa that was facing his counterpart.

'Besides, when you have been in the game for as long as I have, you begin to realise just how many of life's treats are easily obtainable: I have been here three years now and to think that it has taken this long to live in a place like this. I wouldn't be here now without all of my hard work.' Sir Michael sat down opposite his friend. 'Anyway, let's get down to business. My secretary has drafted up some interesting new proposals for the funding of the Police Force. I'm all for making savings here and there but I'm not so sure with this one Peter.'

Peter Dyson, son of Henry Dyson − Civil Servant and Financier to the crown − sat grinning at his elder friend.

'Come now Sir Michael, these are tough times. Money is becoming tight for all of us, not to mention those of us who sit in counting houses. We see profit slip through our fingers on a daily basis and we must comply with the facts that have been presented to us.'

'But cutting the Police Force by 33%? It's madness. With unemployment on the rise and more people joining the dole queue, how on earth can we justify this?'

'Leave it to me Sir Michael. I have orders from the PM that we should go ahead with this plan. And we don't want to get on the PM's bad side now do we?'

Sir Michael sighed. 'Peter, you haven't been in this business as long as I have. We are always made by the press to look like we don't suffer. That it is only the common man who finds himself out of work and we sit on mounds of money, smoking pipes neglecting those we should protect in big houses made of gold.'

'Well, have you seen your surroundings? That doesn't seem like an unfair evaluation!' chuckled Peter.

'Peter, I'm serious. The cuts don't just affect the people who lose their jobs and their families. The senior-ranking members of the organisation in question are forced to take massive pay cuts. The red tops then report to the masses that we take bungs to compensate for this.'

'And they're right,' Peter interrupted.

'Only some, I have never taken a bung. If I had accepted all of those I have been offered in my career I'd be able to afford two houses like this! It's a house of cards and we can't allow it to topple.'

'Listen to me. I can make sure that you will be immune from this. The squeeze is being felt everywhere. Heck, even the billionaires in this world have to cut back. Sir Michael, it will happen: if not now, then a few years down the line.'

'Look at it from my point of view, Peter; if we make cut backs with staff and with the growing unrest in this country, can you imagine the turmoil if the unemployed and the hard done by start rioting? It will be chaos. Youngsters wanting to leave school to become police officers will be turned away. We should be creating jobs not destroying them.'

'Oh dear, I see that you are becoming rather sympathetic to the working classes. Tell me, are you sure that you are with the right political party?'

Sir Michael ignored the snide comment. 'I can understand lowering the funds in a more moderate time frame, but overnight! I'm sorry I just can't let it happen.'

As the old man got up to pour two glasses of port from the drinks cabinet, he knew he wasn't getting through to his younger advisor. He was headstrong, some would say stubborn, but he could not see why the cuts had to be made so suddenly.

The arm of the law had been stretched as far as it could go and the proposed plans would make sure people like him were secure for the future, but the common man?

He was meant to be the figurehead of a very important organisation. He had become a politician so that he could change things for the better, not make them worse. What could he do?

'I can see I'm not getting through to you,' he sighed as he began pouring the drink into the two glass cups.

'Peter, we can't let this happen. We just can't. I mean, who's going to keep the criminals at bay and police sporting events? Think of the Monarchy.'

'It's okay. This new plan will still provide security for the city and the country. It's just going to be tighter. I thought you would be happy to pocket a personal pay check of ten million?'

'I've told you before, I don't bow to bungs and I never will! If you bring that payment up again I shall report you Peter, It's

104

wrong and I won't thank you for trying to bribe my aids either.'

Peter huffed in his comfortable position on the sofa.

He gladly accepted the drink, which he took in his right hand, whilst he fiddled with his jacket pocket with the other, the thick wad of cash chaffing the lining of his shirt, itching to jump out and place itself in Sir Michael's hand.

After a few moments of awkward silence he sipped his drink in a contemplative mood and decided to approach the conversation from a different angle.

'I agree. Truly I do. How can we expect this country's forces to provide the protection we need? I'll tell you how.' He revealed what looked like a letter in a brown envelope.

'So this is what I propose. A new way of policing our country. The PM has a copy, as do some of the loudest voices on the bench. Lords and Ladies have given me their support already, even some celebrities. It isn't out in the public yet, but give it time and it will be.'

'So what you're saying is, if I don't accept the money then I'm out and you take over? Peter for God's sakes what kind of behaviour is this towards one of your friends?'

'The world has changed Sir Michael. You're a few years away from retiring anyway. Why not take it now? Why burden yourself with such a futile stance?'

'I don't believe what I'm hearing. I simply do not *know* what I am hearing.' He put his drink down and began to pace the old room. 'I shall not submit, this isn't the last you have heard of this Peter, now get out before I report you.'

Peter sneered at his old mentor.

'Now!'

'Okay, I'll give you five days to decide. Five days. Then if you still haven't reached a conclusion I'll make it for you. Good day Sir Michael.'

Peter got up from the sofa and made for the door, his glass half full.

Sir Michael also put his drink down to ensure that this traitor - Judas even - left immediately.

His glass was half empty.

As he gazed out of the front door and saw the black cab depart with the police car in tow, his face melted from anger to sadness.

Whichever way he looked at it, he didn't really have a choice. He was a goner.

*

Darkness had fallen in the twenty-five minutes that had elapsed since the meeting. Peter was feeling proud of himself.

106

He had made his stamp on the old bugger and the trap was now set.

With the police force crippled and the man in charge left with no choice but to comply, he had done a very good job indeed. The black cab pulled up in a posh part of the city.

The police car passed it on the road and the sirens went silent. Departing his taxi, Peter searched for the keys to his bachelor pad. Upon finding them, he walked up the two steps to his black door. After opening it, he looked in the mirror.

He smiled at his own dastardly reflection and began to laugh at himself. As he wheeled away, he threw his coat onto the banister of the stairs and proceeded to the kitchen. Turning on a light switch on the wall, the artificial light revealed a pristine black and white design.

Brimming with confidence, he picked the phone up off the hook and dialled to tell his partner in crime what had happened.

'Michelle?'

'Speaking. How did it go, sir?'

'Very well. I outlined the plans to him. Of course he didn't take to them but he knows the score. I've given him five days. If he hasn't made his mind up by then, we move in and take him out. I want you to organise a quiet place for him to be on that day, just in case he doesn't play ball.'

107

'Kill him, sir?'

'You catch on quick,' quipped Peter 'Yes of course kill him. God Michelle!'

'Alright Sir, I'm sorry, busy day.'

'If you don't feel that you are up to it, I can always find someone else who is.'

Michelle panicked a little on the other end of the line.

'No, no it's fine. I'll work things my end and try and make him see sense. I'm sure I can be persuasive.'

Peter laughed and began pouring himself a glass of red wine with his free left hand.

'Good girl. Ring me at midday tomorrow. Speak then.'

Before she could reply, Peter hung up on her. He felt like he was swimming in a sea of power.

He chuckled to himself again and left the kitchen, turning the light off as he went. He walked through the dark hallway and to the living room.

Sitting down in the dark in his favourite chair, he turned the lamp light on, only to reveal that he wasn't the only person in the room.

'Sounds like you've had a good day at the office. Care to share the good news?'

Peter froze like a rabbit in the headlights. He looked at the man who sat in the opposite chair to him, gun in his hand and starring intensively with puppy dog blue eyes.

'I'm afraid I don't talk to strangers,' Peter answered, putting his drink down on the table next to his chair.

'I insist.'

'Oh, well that's different then. You have got a nerve breaking in here. Let me guess: around the back? The unknown man barely blinked.

'Well I'd like to know where I need a little more security around the house.'

'Peter Dyson, former Civil Servant and professional entrepreneur, otherwise known as lapdog and long term right hand man to the Big Chief. One question. Why the name Black Diamond?'

Peter laughed. 'I'm sorry I think you've got the wrong person.'

'Black Diamond. A name that has gone under the radar due to the mysterious nature of the man who owns it. The man has a thirty year track record of murder, embezzlement and conspiracy that has led to the deaths of not just innocent people but of those in certain parts of the establishment and influential figures who could have made a difference over the years.'

'Never heard of him. Now please, if you can just leave before I call the police.'

'That's funny, from what I know there won't be many policeman around anymore to answer prank calls,' the unknown man smiled out of the corner of his mouth, his arm still rigid with the gun in his hand, steadily aimed at Peter's head.

'How did you know that?'

'You've got a mole in Sir Michael's office. We have got one in yours.'

'Michelle? The bitch!'

'No, not Michelle. Although don't think she will get away with this either. That note, what was in it?'

'I can't tell you.' Peter's throat began to feel dry.

'Try.'

Peter raised the glass up to his lips and began to sip. At that point, he kicked the gun out of the unknown man's hand, causing a shot to be buried in the wall above his head. Peter dropped to the floor, scrambling for the gun in the dim light but the unknown man had launched himself on the floor also and began tussling with the Black Diamond on the floor.

The Black Diamond had strength that defied his middle age and he landed a couple of blows in his trespassers ribcage.

110

The unknown man winced a little. The injuries he had picked up from the attack in the woods still hadn't healed fully and any further damage would result in more time off.

It's a miracle that after a few days stay with the lonely lady in the cottage he was able to return to duty, but his superior had wanted him to rest up for another week, leaving him itching to get back to work. If he was being truthful to himself, another week would have done the trick, but he couldn't let Black Diamond get away after he heard what was being planned. It's a good thing that there were spies on both sides.

The struggle was dispersed with punches from both parties until the unknown man gained the upper hand and reclaimed his gun, pointing it at the scared bloody face of the man who he was on top of.

'No more fun time. I want answers and I want them now damn it! You will tell me everything I want to know and correctly!'

The Black Diamond, now resembling more of a black and blue diamond, gasped for air after the struggle. 'Alright, alright!'

The unknown man picked up his prisoner and threw him back in the chair. Without taking an eye off him, the unknown man resumed his position on the opposite chair.

'The Big Chief, who is he?'

111

'But he'll kill me.'

'Tell me!'

'He is the man who controls all of the organised crime in this country. His network goes back decades and even the PM is afraid of him.'

The unknown man cocked his gun. 'I don't think you understood the question. Who. Is. HE?'

The Black Diamond jumped. 'I can't tell you. He head hunted me twenty-five years ago. I was just a newly elected backbencher, keen to make my mark and more money. When I heard that there was an organisation that could promise me more money and power I worked for them behind my constituency's back.'

'Lost funds, lack of a governing body. It's a miracle you stayed in power, you're still not answering my question but we will get there. So the Big Chief protected you?'

'Yes, I did some favours for him and he did some for me. He gave me the code name Black Diamond because it meant that my criminal activities were hard to trace back to me.'

'The things you gave the stamp of approval for: bombings in town centres, the murders of your closest rivals in Parliament. Good honest people died, and for what? For scum like you to walk away with another million in your back pocket. You make me sick.'

The Black Diamond leaned forward, nursing a cut to his forehead.

'Don't you dare lecture me, you're no better.'

'I do the job the police can't do. I make sure people like you pay for what they have done; the despised and unworthy always get their come-uppance.'

'I know, we know all about you, young man, AND your organisation. We had moles working in your secret company for months. If we're going down we shall take you lot with us!'

The unknown man seemed unfazed by this news. Even if this man did truly know who he was, it was a fake file anyway.

Nobody knew who he was, not even his own Superior, not really. He liked it that way.

'You're good, but not that good: we take you out of the picture then the Big Chief's empire begins to crack. We know how damaging not getting The Boss and GEMINI's backing was to you. Don't pretend otherwise. It's true, for a number of years your organisation has been a muddy sponge, sucking up the dirty small time Charlie's just so the Big Chief can have more and more power. You see this is what happens when the poor become poorer. They fight back.'

'You don't have any proof,' the Black Diamond said.

'Think about what you are saying. We have copies of this supposed new deal to revolutionise the police force. Basically, it looks like from taking it over you'll turn the force into an unstoppable gang of thugs, is that correct?'
Black Diamond nodded.

'So, in order to do this, you have to dispose of Sir Michael Houghton first, is that so?'

'Yes, what of it?'

'To put you in charge, getting your hands dirty for the Big Chief again.'

'Much in the same way as you do for your boss.'
The unknown man's eyes grew red with anger. 'Don't you dare compare me to you. The people I kill have committed terrible crimes. I'm just taking the rubbish out.'

'What are you going to do to me? Are you going to hand me over?'

'To get the facts that we need, we'll have to be very thorough with our questioning.'

'No, you will not torture me. I will never give in to you scumbags!'

The unknown man's stare cut instantly to a friendlier look and he lowered his firearm.

'Ah, well that's alright then, come on mate we'll take care of you.'

'What?'

'Yeah, it's okay, we won't hurt you anymore.'

Black Diamond couldn't believe what he was hearing. Was this the same man who had broken in, assaulted and terrorized him?

Black Diamond laughed. 'You see, I knew you wouldn't do that to such a wealth of information as me.'

The unknown man laughed out loud and threw his head back.

'Of course not, do you want to know why?'

'Ha-ha, why?' enquired Black Diamond, giggling to himself.

'Well, that would be pointless after we have broken into your house and already obtained the information.' The unknown man's expression went back to its previous serious state and he levelled his gun once more.

Black Diamond's sudden pleas were silenced as five bullets nestled into his body. The fifth, which hit him in the head, kept travelling into the back of his chair and the exit wound spouted bits of red and pink clumps, which were once his warped brain. The unknown man had done his job. Black Diamond was no more. By taking another piece out of the picture, his firm was further crippling the Big Chief's empire.

It was all about taking out one cinder block at a time until the whole building came down. The unknown man watched as the corpse slumped bloodily to the floor. He kicked it hard when it was lying in a mess on the cream carpet.

Another one down, not many more to go, he thought.

The unknown man looked up at the window.　It's a good thing that he had already closed the curtains in the house before the Black Diamond got home and that the evil man had ignored it in his smug state. All he had to do now was pick up the evidence and cover his tracks. He left the living room and made for the oven.

Opening the door, he turned the gas on and then proceeded to walk upstairs. At the top of the stairs he saw some lights reflect through the curtains.

He glanced down at his watch. 08:07, thirteen minutes to go.

Smiling, the unknown man made for the converted room that was now dressed out as an office. Picking up the villain's diary and other files, he put them in a black plastic carrier bag, which he produced from his pocket.

He swiped all the files and boxes full of paper. He had already looked at these earlier, records of all the Big Chief's big jobs from the past fifteen years.

Tying a knot in the bag, he slung it over his shoulder. He didn't feel at all bad about the running gas. The way the house was built meant that it was a good few yards from any neighbouring residents, so they wouldn't be harmed. Startled yes, but unharmed. He made his way back downstairs, the hiss of the free gas swelling in the kitchen.

He looked down at his watch, 08:12. Still three minutes to go. He could still breathe but the air was becoming more toxic.

He retraced his steps to the living room and stepped over the dead body of a terrible criminal. Gazing down on the prone figure, he wondered about all the suffering Black Diamond had caused over the years and the threat to Sir Michael's life.

'I hope you like it well done,' he quipped producing a set of matches from the same pocket the black bag had been in.

He raced through to the conservatory and put on a balaclava that had been inside his other jacket pocket. Putting it on over his head, he took to the half open conservatory window, which had provided his entry route (what a stupid man to be so negligent, he thought) and held the matches in his hand whilst placing the bag outside. He would have to be quick. Striking the match, he threw it as far as he could, hoping the toxic air would catch it before it went out. It did.

As the unknown man leapt through the window, a tremendous explosion ripped through the house, blowing glass from the windows and sending a fireball surging through the rooms.

The unknown man covered his hands and head and lay in a foetal position a few yards away.

The force of the explosion had blown him clear across the garden and he fell on his cargo in the black sack. As soon as the worst of the explosion had passed, he picked himself up, then retrieved the bag with the information in it and ran for the garden gate.

He ran along the back pathway that led into a local park, he could hear shocked screams from people nearby. Where he was running was quiet and deserted so he assumed that the commotion was happening at the front of the burning house. Running as fast as he could, he took the balaclava off and came off the back road and back onto the main one. His breath stabilising out of a sprint-induced pant, he walked calmly past a few people, who were running towards the burning house.

Without looking back, he could picture the scene and it wouldn't be pretty. Happily for him, he spotted the black Mercedes parked just beyond the corner of the street.

Opening the boot and throwing the black bag inside, he then closed the boot and opened the rear door just as the engine started. Looking to his left, he saw his superior sitting next to him.

'You do like to cause a commotion don't you?'

'Not normally, but this time, I wanted to make sure that nothing could be salvaged,' he wiped his brow as the driver took the handbrake off and slipped inconspicuously into the night.

'Michelle?' The unknown man inquired. 'Did you find her?

'She's coming in tonight. So, did you get everything?'

'Yes, I had most of the afternoon to look through what information he had. It's all in the boot,' the unknown man smiled.

'The Big Chief, We have got him, Sir.'

CHAPTER SEVEN

RELEASE THE TIGERS

'Illegal move'

Brett Larsson wiped a bead of sweat from his brow as he stared at the decimated chessboard. He picked the white knight up and shakily put it back in its original position. He didn't have a clue how he was losing so badly.

Up until now, Brett had been the champion chess player in the country. He had planned to use his skill as a way to make friends when he first moved to England from his native Sweden twelve years previously.

Since then, he had gained a reputation as a poker faced, never-say-die competitor, who had harnessed his talent into a sure-fire way of making a living.

The award money he picked up was never enough, as his greed wouldn't allow that.

Winning chess matches was his way of making big money off other, less capable and talented fools.

Slowly but surely a reputation engulfed his being. Stories began to circulate and his wealth soared through the roof. As time had moved on, the stakes had grown steadily higher and what had started out as a nice little earner on the side had transformed Brett into an egocentric. Now it wasn't all about the money. It was all about power.

He had played and beaten fellow champions from around the world, businessmen and even members of the English Monarchy – although that was only ever for charity events that increased his reputation. In fact, it was an article in a broadsheet newspaper that had brought him to the attention of the man he faced at that precise moment. The offer had been too good to refuse.

Both men were to put five million pounds of their own money on the table and the winner takes all.

The approach was made in a letter to his personal correspondents. He was told to come alone to the chosen location, the old church hall in the centre of town, at half ten the next day. Brett had pondered on whether to take the stranger up on his offer. The excitement and mystery thrilled him.

He had grown weary of his previous tournaments; it was as if the game of chess was becoming rather dull. He didn't think of the danger that it might bring so he bounded off into the night, certain that the fortune would be his by the next evening.

He had checked his funds, he had enough to meet the wager but it was scraping the barrel. Still, his own personal fortune would be doubled and he could retire to a far-flung country. Also, the name the man had given to him brought a further sense of mystery to the proceedings. It was as if Brett was in a spy film. However, in his current predicament, he really wished he hadn't accepted the invitation.

He looked up at his opponent, who grinned through the shadows in front of him. The man's pearly white teeth shone through the darkness. Brett had found it superstitious that only one light dangling high above them was aglow, while the others hung as dark as a murderers mind.

'Another move like that and I'll be convinced that you're an imposter. This isn't the Brett Larsson I have heard of. Try again.'

Brett shook off his opponent's mockery. He looked to his left and his right. Two well-built men stood watching him, the only other people in the auditorium. The light swung in time to the air conditioning that swirled in the darkness. Slowly but surely, Brett moved the same white knight two squares to the right. It was the only other move he could make. There were only two other pieces still on the board for him.

The queen and a rook stared at the black pieces that threatened to engulf them. The stranger's own black army of pieces had a few casualties, but in a little over fifteen minutes he was ready to strike the fatal blow and claim his ten million.

'Checkmate.'

The whites of Brett's eyes grew larger with that final, terrible statement. He looked down on the dirty, aged chessboard. The white queen was vanquished. The game was over and Brett had lost his first match in over a decade.

'How? How?! Nobody can beat me, no one!'

'The evidence suggests otherwise,' said the stranger in his deep, Scottish accent. 'Still, you put up a good fight.' The stranger in the shadows reached out to Brett's side of the table and gleefully proceeded to collect the suitcase, which was by his side.

'I'll be taking my winnings now, and I suggest you leave before I decide to take more.'

'What? Don't you know who I am? I am the champion of the world. This was obviously some kind of set-up. You've cheated.'

124

Brett didn't take at all kindly to his defeat. His head was awash with excuses. The lighting had thrown him off his game. The unfamiliar surroundings had disturbed him. The growing sense of realisation that his opponent was a very dangerous man also contributed to his lack of success during the match.

'Are you accusing me of cheating?' the stranger's voice, menacing yet eloquent, beckoned for an answer through the dark. 'If anything it should be me who should be accusing you. I thought I was playing the best of the best, yet it turns out it is I who has been conned.'

Brett put his hand on the suitcase's handle, snapping it away from the strangers grasp.

'We had a deal Mr. Larsson; I suggest you stand by it.'

The sweat trickled down Brett's nose, the air conditioning doing nothing for his perspiration.

'Why what are you going to do? It's a chess game god damn it! Some creep who feels the need to be protected by a couple of thugs will not threaten me.'

The stranger smashed his fist down upon the old table making the sound echo around the old church hall. 'Don't you dare cross me. I can't guarantee what I would do in retaliation would be pleasant.'

Brett completely lost his temper and stood up bending over the table and shouted into the stranger's face.

'Who do you think you are?'

The stranger also leant forward and was now so close to Brett's face he could feel the hot musk of sweat on his face.

'I am the Big Chief,' he said, looking closely into his opponent's eyes. 'And you have lost the game.'

The look in Brett's eyes changed from one of anger to one of sheer terror. He had heard about this man from some of his gambling circles. He had to get out and fast. Dropping the suitcase like a boulder in the sand, Brett panicked and stumbled back. At that same moment the Big Chief, who stared down upon his beaten opponent, clicked his fingers.

The thugs, who had been standing obediently beside him, were allowed off their leash and they walked at a pace towards the cowering Brett.

One produced a knife from his jacket pocket and Brett became hysterical.

'No! No! Keep away from me!' the terrified Scandinavian crawled towards the door, just a few metres away. In one scoop, the goons picked him up and dragged him, kicking and screaming like a child having a tantrum into the main part of the church.

The Big Chief stood silently, his temper cooling in the dark room. As he collected his things, both briefcases and his long dark coat, the screams of fear shrieked into a blood-curdling scream that pierced the shadows. The Big Chief remained silent and was not affected by the cold murder that had happened next door. When he was ready, he turned for the door, with no remorse or thought towards the man he had just sentenced to death.

The two henchmen appeared from the shadows, one cleaning his knife with a cloth, and then they too departed the lonely church into the night.

Outside, a car was waiting by the gates to the house of God. The Big Chief pulled his coat up in the cool night air. It was a clear yet cloudy night and his features blended in with the night sky.

The two henchmen had caught up with their superior and one politely opened the door to allow his boss in the car. The classic black Rolls Royce was upholstered with a creamy finish inside and the Big Chief settled himself down next to the figure of a woman who occupied the other passenger seat.

'I'm so sorry that took so long.'

The girl, who was roughly in her mid twenties, brushed the long blonde hair out of her face, which revealed a face that was pretty yet contorted with fear.

'What's wrong young lady?'

The girl began to stutter, her mouth dry with nervousness.

'Sir, I'm afraid I...I have some bad news.'

The Big Chief scowled in his seat as the second henchman closed his master's door and leapt in the front passenger seat. The car squealed into life and departed the church.

'Go on.'

The girl swallowed a lump in her throat.

'I have news that Black Diamond is dead.'

The Big Chief, who had been leaning forward towards the girl, collapsed back in his seat.

'It was him, wasn't it?'

The girl nodded, too frightened to make eye contact with her boss.

'How did he die?'

'It looks like he was trapped in a fire in his house, we can't be sure if he was already dead but I do know that our target was assigned to carry out the murder.'

'Did he take anything from the house?'

The girl hesitated. She wasn't sure what to say.

'DID THEY TAKE ANYTHING?' screamed the Big Chief, his eyes brimming with anger.

The girl looked to her left and saw that look in his eyes. Not many had seen that look and lived.

128

'I don't know. It only happened a couple of hours ago.'

The Big Chief recoiled, still staring at the girl.

'If he did then they know my plans already. How many of our spies have been found within their organisation?'

'I am the last, Sir.'

The Big Chief clenched his fist in rage. He was not used to feeling this vulnerable.

'Then time moves against us. Do you think they suspect you?'

'I don't think so. Unless…'

'Unless the others have told them of your true identity,' interrupted the Big Chief.

Ever since GEMINI and the boss had been obliterated, his plans for complete network domination had fallen into ruins.

He knew who was behind it, so the Big Chief had sent his spies who had been working within the Secret Service's firm to finish the unknown man off.

However, his plan had failed. How, after so many years of every detail being finalized and very single plan concluding faultlessly, could everything suddenly begin to turn?

'Then we have no time to lose. Tonight you will go back to the organization and find out everything you can about this assassin. Use every skill you have to get into their records and get out as soon as you have the information we need.'

129

The girl gasped. 'Sir, I can't go back there now, they will find me. Besides, we already have some of his details. Haven't we got enough to go on?'

'You will go back there tonight and get in touch with your contact as soon as you have the information. Put the file in a bag, you can even take pictures if you want, I don't give a toss. Just get me everything you can on that man. I want to hit him hard and fast!'

'But don't we already know who he is?'

'I don't know enough. If we can't kill him I want to get him where it hurts. Look up bank statements, old lovers, where he lives, everything. Be thorough and use your contact when you are done. Get in and out as fast as you can. If you are caught before you get your hands on the details then I am finished. I can't let that happen. We will drop you off at the offices. Be discreet, but use that body of yours if you need to get past anybody.'

The girl didn't take this as a compliment. She was scared for her safety. She had heard what had happened to the other spies who had been caught. She wouldn't be able to stand up to that kind of treatment.

'Am I making myself clear?' The Big Chief spoke to his associate but didn't look at her. He was lost in the scenery out of his window. He owned this city and he wanted it to stay that way.

'Yes,' the girl nodded. She opened her handbag and rummaged around for her pass.

She looked at the card. *Hannah Warren; Secretary*. She put the card, which was on a chain, around her neck and checked her reflection in the mirror in her purse.

The Big Chief ignored this moment of vanity and continued his pitch.

'If we can take this sod down then they are finished. I already have everything on them except how I can deal with this mystery man. I am set to release the tigers on them as it were. They have killed Black Diamond. An eye for an eye. I don't even care about the old fart that runs the place. He will be dealt with soon enough. Just get me the details and we're back up and running.'

'Yes, Sir.'

The car swooped around a corner. The streets were busy even if it was getting late. The classic Rolls Royce pulled up on the side of the pavement and slowed to a halt.

The Big Chief pulled himself away from the window and glared at the girl.

'Showtime,' he hissed.

The girl nodded nervously and opened the door. She stepped out onto the street and the black Rolls Royce pulled away. They had dropped her off a couple of streets away from the organization's offices. It would create suspicion if they were seen to be dropping her off right on their doorstep. Inhaling hard, the girl put her coat on and swung her handbag onto her shoulder.

Tonight was the night when she had a date with destiny. Either she carried out her task and succeeded or she would be thrown to the wolves and her life would no longer be worth living.

Walking towards the office, a cool exterior shone about her person. Inside, her heartbeat grew faster. If she failed, the Big Chief would release the tigers on her. She had her target in sights.

The unknown man was going to pay for what he had done.

CHAPTER EIGHT

ESCAPE SWITCH

Hannah Warren moved quickly in the dark library. She had been surprised at how easy it was to break in to the offices at night. The guards who normally adorned the front door were nowhere to be seen and the night workers were especially sporadic.

Maybe they had been given the night off in celebration of the death of Black Diamond, she thought. She had tried not to provoke suspicion among the few people who had remained in the building late into the night, so she walked with her usual coolness and had gained easy access to the organization's library of records.

It was all in the dusty, vast room: every case, every person who had been found out by the Secret Service's never-ending network of spies and agents. The room was so big and full of case notes that Hannah had always joked that the Service had been around since the beginning of time itself.

As she continued along the long dark corridor she produced a torch from her handbag. The torch, which was no more than a couple of inches long, was discreet and not bright enough to alert the whole building to her presence. She had left the main lights off so that she would not be detected.

The company had become increasingly insecure about their security since the massive breach not long ago. About a dozen or so spies had been revealed since the unknown man was attacked by a group of them nearly seven weeks previously. Hannah had dealt with the log on the incident.

He had been in a physically bad way, yet was clever enough not to tell his superior where he was – otherwise Hannah could have alerted the Big Chief to his location and the last obstacle before total domination would have been hurdled.

Hannah's torch pierced the dark like a knife through hot butter. She remembered the way since she had memorized it in her eleven months working as a double agent. But if she were to obtain the important file then she'd have to know that she had stolen the correct one, and with her eyesight, there would be no way that she could ever read it in the dark.

Hannah's flat shoes made no sound as they walked down the endless rows of records. Even she wouldn't be so stupid as to wear high heels that clip-clopped her way into detection.

She sporadically looked over her shoulder and betrayed her instincts. She had been a confident, level-headed girl until tonight because she knew that if she were caught, it would be the end of her.

After what seemed like an age of lurking through the library she turned to her right and her big blue eyes shone in the night as she glimpsed at the filing cabinet labelled *Employees*.

'Finally,' she whispered to herself.

Even though the name of her target wasn't known to anybody, his likeness would be on record and she knew where it was within the tall cabinet. The old and rusty metal winced its way open as she tugged on the handle, revealing dozens of tightly packed files on the employees of the Secret Service.

She flicked through, remembering that she had hidden the file ten rungs back in the drawer. She had dealt with the file only a few days before and unless someone else had decided to get the file out, it should still be there.

Her fingers wrapped around the tenth file and wrenched it from the tightly packed contents of the filing cabinet draw. She already knew that she would not obtain the information that she craved – the truth behind the unknown man's identity.

Even the Secret Service wouldn't be so stupid to list their top assassin's real names. She did spot a yellowing, crumbling sticker over the top of where the name would be, but upon peeling it back slightly, Hannah noticed that a name had been present but it had been obliterated by an indelible pen.

However, other personal information was on file, such as next of kin, blood type and age. She crouched down onto the cold metal floor and flicked the file's cover over.

There he was.

The face of a killer stared back at her through the page. Dark hair, puppy dog blue eyes and a lined face. It was him alright. She looked at his codename. Unlisted. What? Even the unknown man does not have a codename. She hadn't noticed that before, even though she had handled the file herself on a few occasions.

How could she miss that detail? Did that mean that even the firm didn't trust this man? Or that his identity was so precious to him that he hadn't told even his employers? Surely that meant that even they were scared of him.

She continued her search through the thick file. She computed the highlights.

53 Kills in ten years

6.9 cases closed thanks to agent's interventions

Injured in action on seven occasions, permanent damage to left shoulder after the Columbine incident.

Commended in the organization's history as greatest assassin.

Currently assigned to the case of the Big Chief – case two years in progress.

Next of Kin ...Smith

Eureka! He has a wife! Or a girlfriend? Did this mean that his last name was Smith? That's a bit boring after all the mystery he has surrounded himself in. She produced a small camera from her handbag and proceeded to photograph every page.

They had him.

After several minutes of photographing, Hannah was interrupted by the sound of the library door opening. She jumped and hurriedly put the file back together again before forcing it in no particular order back in the drawer.

'Anybody in here?'

She recognized the voice. It was Dave the security guard. He was a nice approachable fellow, a bit old and fat for Hannah's tastes, but she liked him. She could use this to her advantage.

'Only me Dave,' she cooed through the murky air.

'Hannah. What are you doing here so late at night?'

She called back whilst putting the drawer back in its rusty cabinet.

'I was working late. Just filing some information away, I didn't turn the lights on because I didn't want it to look suspicious. I'm sorry.'

'That's okay Miss,' Dave smiled as he saw Hannah's slim, sexy figure slide towards him out of the shadows. 'I didn't know that you were so dedicated to the job.'

Hannah smiled and giggled. 'I'm full of surprises, me.'

Dave laughed. 'I bet you are! After you Miss.'

He made a gesture with his hand as if to usher her out of the massive library. She smiled nervously again and departed followed by the security guard. As they walked down the long corridor towards the main offices they chatted further.

'Got any plans for the weekend Miss?'

'Not much, seeing the boyfriend for a bit Saturday night. Apart from that it's going to be a quiet one. What about you Dave?'

'Got to take the wife and kids to see my mum, apart from that the usual, not being allowed to watch what I want to watch on the box and not getting a lie-in,' Dave chuckled to himself.

'Anyway I'd better be locking up soon.'

'Oh, just give me ten minutes. I just need to get something out of my locker,' Hannah tore herself away from the leisurely stroll and ran back down the corridor.

'Okay, but be quick Miss,' Dave smiled at her and watched as she turned around the corner and out of view.

Immediately, Dave's smile disappeared from his lips and he reached for the walkie-talkie on his utility belt.

'Sir, you may want to get down here. Something suspicious is going on.'

*

Hannah sprinted towards the locker room and nervously rummaged in her handbag for her locker key. She had pre-arranged for her contact to pick up the camera from her locker the next day.

She may be the last spy within the complex, but when her contact poses as a cleaner and picks up the information the Big Chief so badly needed, it meant that if she were caught, then the information would still make its way back to her boss, who she feared in abundance. She gulped hard at the thought of being found out.

She had heard the stories of what had happened to the other moles in the firm and she knew they would show no mercy, even towards a young girl.

She placed the camera under some spare clothes and shut the door, locking the metal locker after her. She took a deep breath and wheeled away towards the main door.

She was so close to escape, she could taste the reward. No more pretending. This was to be the last time she would ever step foot in the building and the best thing about it was she had got away when everybody else had been captured.

The Big Chief would be very pleased with her. She had succeeded.

'Okay Dave, I'm ready now.' Hannah looked down as she fiddled with her coat and draped her handbag over her shoulder. A few paces later, Dave had not answered.

'Dave?'

Hannah turned into the main hall, where the doors to freedom waited for her. As she looked up, her escape route was blocked – for there stood her superior, two men in dark clothing and Dave, who looked at her with a sense of betrayal.

'Going somewhere Miss Warren?'

Hannah's mind panicked. Shit, so near. They had her. The Big Chief had his information and she was now in the jaws of the people she was really working against.

The last spy, caught in the net. Dave had been watching her since she came in and reported to his superior, whose usual friendly face was replaced with a cold look of anger.

'I think you should come with me.' The superior's two guards walked towards her and picked her up.

'Let go of me, I've done nothing wrong! Where are you taking me?' Hannah protested as she was frog marched out of the main hall and away for unknown terrors to face at the hands of her victims.

'That's the last one Dave,' said the superior, who noticed the look of hurt on his face 'You can go home now, you can go home. Leave the keys with me and I'll clean up. Have a good weekend and I'll see you Monday,' he patted Dave on the shoulder in a friendly gesture.

'Good night, sir,' Dave made for the door. Looking back, he watched as the Superior followed the protesting Hannah. That was to be the last time Dave saw his colleague and he knew what happened next.

'Poor Hannah. Poor, poor Hannah.'

141

CHAPTER NINE

NOTHING ELSE MATTERS

There is nothing in this world less welcoming than the home of an assassin. The unknown man always knew that when his life changed, this fact would mean he would have to cut all the more pleasurable aspects of his old life out.

The sacrifices he had made had hurt him badly and his superior knew it. But it had made him the best agent they had at the Service and that mattered more than anything if it meant the end of the Big Chief, the cancer of the country who had to be cut out before the nation died.

He had lied to himself that it was worth it: that nothing else mattered.

He had recently begun to think that he was just an insignificant piece really. When he carried out his final task of killing the Big Chief, there would be no recognition, no fanfare. Who'd applaud a killer but fellow murderers?

He knew that he had become as a big a piece of social scum as his enemies. And it hurt.

143

He kept himself to himself in the sky-reaching block of luxurious apartments. The view allowed the inhabitants of the higher rungs of the block to feel like kings looking down upon their empire and yet, as he gazed at the twinkling car headlights of the far away cars and the bright lights of the city, the unknown man felt less than triumphant.

Leaning against the glass door that enveloped onto his personal box, he cradled a glass of Jack Daniels in his hand, solemnly lost in his thoughts.

He had killed again and it hadn't make him feel good. It never made him feel good.

He was going soft; maybe it had been the attack in the woods that had done it to him. Or maybe a decade of being a clinical and calculating assassin had worn thin and he was thinking about his old life again – pinning for the return of the person he once was.

When he thought back to how he was just as he joined the service, it was like looking at the life of a completely different person.

The apartment hadn't always been empty. There was a point, years ago, when the unknown man could use his name without fear, never had to look over his shoulder and after a hard day at the office he could fall back into the arms of his loved one and live the life of a normal person.

The unknown man stared through eyes swimming in melancholy.

The dark night outside suddenly melted away before his eyes and he saw before him a mirage of his past life. He saw visions of himself as a much younger man, his face clean-shaven with no deep lines brought about by stress and strain.

Then, in his mind's eye, he saw Rachel. It was as if she were back in the room with him. She was a slim figured woman, black hair in a bob that bounced around her slender neck, and when her lips parted in a wide smile it used to melt the unknown man's heart. She was the only person in the world who he loved.

Ah, how the unknown man remembered that first meeting.

*

He had been in the company for a couple of years at the rank of Civil Agent. It was nowhere near as dangerous as his current vocation but it was still a job that needed doing. He was employed by the Government to conduct takeovers of businesses that had fallen behind in standards.

He'd been to banks and major department stores. It had been a good job to have after coming out of University but his life was a lonely one. He had moved into the city in a flat above a shop and he longed for a partner.

Then, one day, his superior introduced him to Rachel Smith.

He had fallen in love instantly and he remembered how stunned he was by her beauty on that first meeting.

'Pleased to meet you, Mrs. Smith,' he said smiling broadly.

'Um, it's Miss actually. It's nice to meet you too.'

Rachel's eyes were big and wide. If he stared for long enough, the unknown man could fall into their alluring gaze.

'Rachel's just transferred here from Scotland,' his superior had said.

'That's funny; you don't have an accent, how come?'

'I have just qualified with a first in Business Studies from the University of Edinburgh; I've been told you went to University too?'

The unknown man looked down, still smiling. He felt slightly silly.

'Yes I have, I graduated from Manchester University. Who told you I'd been to University?'

The superior looked away.

'Oh I see,' chuckled the unknown man. He knew this was a set up. He'd not known his superior for long, but it was obvious to him who was playing matchmaker here.

'Miss Smith will join you on your next assignment' he said, looking back at the young couple. 'I thought that you could show her the ropes as it were, especially since you will be working very closely together'.

'That a brilliant idea,' exclaimed the unknown man.

His enthusiasm made Rachel giggle awkwardly.

He's cute, she thought, and funny.

'I think we are going to get on very well,' she said holding her hand out to her new partner.

'Me too,' the unknown man replied and shook her hand and watched as she followed his superior out of the tiny office he occupied and into the corridor. He wrote in his diary that sat with the mass of paperwork on his desk. It was a Tuesday and in the section for Friday he wrote:

FRIDAY 17TH: ASK RACHEL OUT FOR A DRINK AND BUY HER SOME FLOWERS.

*

As the unknown man laughed to himself at the memory he took a swig of his Jack Daniels and went over to the stereo. He switched it on at the wall and let the record that was on the needle play automatically.

147

As he reclined into the armchair the memories began to play again in his head like a movie reel. He had asked Rachel out that Friday and although she seemed embarrassed by the proposal and made him wait a couple of hours for her reply, she finally walked into his office and said, 'Why not?'

Why not. Those were the two best words he had heard all day.

'Well, could have been worse,' he said to himself as she left the office. 'It could have been sod off!'

That evening he had taken Rachel for dinner at a local Italian restaurant. After that, they went to see a film and he did the gentlemanly thing and paid for her fare back home. She had been flattered that he hadn't taken advantage of her on the first date and for that, she agreed to see him again the week after. It soon became clear to the people within their department that there was more than a professional relationship occurring between them.

Nobody seemed to care; they all seemed to be swept up in the couple's obvious happiness.

The unknown man sat back, taking another swig of his drink as he let the record play.

*

As *Sunshine of Your Love* by Cream swelled in the dark living room, he closed his eyes and let the memories continue to flood back. Although it felt as if he was walking over his own grave, he allowed the past to break down the door in his mind that had been locked.

*

Within two years, his relationship with Rachel had become more serious and they had found a spacious apartment overlooking the city, which they moved into very soon after the second anniversary of their first meeting. He had already started wondering if Rachel was THE one. They had it all. They both had very well paid jobs that were paying their University debts off quickly and now they had their first home together.

Life was looking rosy for the first time since he lost his parents in a terrible terrorist bombing when he was a child. They would have been so proud of their son now and he took comfort from that. Then, one day not long after he began thinking about proposing to her, a job offer came up.

His superior had seen the unknown man's prowess with a weapon on a team-building hunting trip.

149

There was a position that had come up and although it may not be a pleasant one, the pay rise would be astronomical and he would become the company's greatest asset. He was called into his superior's office on the top floor and given the brief. They wanted him to become more than just a Civil Agent.

They wanted him to become a Secret Service Agent. The company was, after all, a cover for a corporation that operated for Her Majesty's Government and he knew that – he had even been required to sign the Secrets Act before taking on his job, just in case he let the cat out of the bag. But nothing had prepared him for how serious the organisation's real work was.

Was he really cut out for that line of work?

More importantly, if he had to, could he even contemplate taking another person's life?

'What me, a secret agent? Sir, everyone can hear when I drop a cup in the kitchen at work.'

'Come on son, it's an honour to be given such an opportunity. You are young and just the person we are looking for. Be honest, you don't want to stay as a Civil Servant for the rest of your days do you?'

'Well no,' he had replied. 'But to kill someone, I can't do that.'

'I'm not going to lie to you. I admire you a lot. Your job may not be around much longer as you know and this is something you should take very seriously. You will be above the law, the biggest sheriff in town. Her Majesty needs you.'

His superior pulled himself out of his comfy chair and proceeded to pace around his office.

'To serve your Queen and country is a job that you should never turn down, no matter how dangerous. My generation laid our lives down to fight for this proud nation to remain independent. Some of them were younger than you. When I started working for this company after the war I felt pride in what I have achieved. And you can achieve so much more than I did.'

'I still don't know, what do I tell Rachel?'

'You tell her nothing for now. I don't want you uttering one word. This is just between you and me for the moment. I will give you a week to think about it.'

His superior had told him to keep the job offer quiet from his girlfriend and to consider the opportunity, and the pressure from such a secret soon began to eat away at him. After a brief period of consideration, the unknown man decided to go for it. If he didn't like it then surely he could just resign?

Then what? He could just be honest with Rachel and seek another job somewhere. When he accepted the offer and signed the contract, the training began, and not knowing how to tell his beloved Rachel, he kept the new job from her. The case they had worked on had finished a long time ago and they were now in separate departments anyway so she wouldn't notice his absence at work if the training overran.

Sometimes he questioned to himself just how innocent she was: surely she knew what the company's real duty was?

He had no idea that it would be the beginning of the end of their young love affair. Rachel started having concerns about her lover. He was spending less time with her and his usual casual manner had become more efficient. It was as if it was a different person that was coming home to her in the evenings.

She had even started talking to fellow friends about how much he had changed. At first they suggested that he was having an affair.

Impossible, she thought, because he would have shown shame when coming home late at night.

He wasn't even coming home late enough to be shagging somebody else's girlfriend and if it was somebody at work she was pretty sure that she would have known. No, it wasn't an affair. It was as if someone had turned a switch off in his head.

Maybe he was being made to do something he didn't want to. She had to find out.

Rachel decided to confront him about it that evening. It had caused an argument. The unknown man had become tetchy and accused her of thinking he was being unfaithful. His anger petrified her. She had never seen him in such a rage.

Fearful for her safety, she locked herself in the bathroom and sobbed uncontrollably on the cold cream floor.

This was the man who she wanted to have a family with one day. She loved him so much and he had changed so much in such a small space of time.

When they started dating, he had told her that his parents had died years earlier and that he had been brought up by his strict Grandparents, and she had felt sorry for him – but now she was worried that those difficult days had triggered a depression inside him. Rachel screamed at him for him to leave her alone and the flat instantly became eerily quiet.

After the incident had calmed down, she looked at the mess that her make-up had made on her face. As she touched up her mascara, she heard the phone ring.

The unknown man picked it up almost instantly and his cool exterior soon returned.

153

'Hello…Yes Sir…Tonight? But it seems too soon…No, no I'm ready, where is he? Okay, I'll get on the road and report back to you later this evening.'

Rachel unlocked the door and looked across the hallway at her loved one slumped in his chair. He stared at the phone, as if someone had just given him bad news. As he approached him he sensed her coming closer and cleared his throat.

'It's err…the boss; he wants me to go back to the office. I'll be back shortly.'

'What, at this hour?'

'Yes, it's very important apparently. I'm so sorry about earlier, we'll talk later.'

'Darling, what happened to you?' she threw her arms around his neck and held him in them.

He slumped back into them, feeling her warm embrace. He was going to need all the strength he could muster tonight.

He turned to his forgiving girlfriend and kissed her passionately. He regretted everything that had just happened and he hated to make her upset.

'I promise I won't be long. If you are awake when I get back then we'll have a talk.'

'So, there is something troubling you? Darling, please tell me what it is?'

He looked into her begging eyes and they melted his heart. It was starting to get cold where his love had once burned bright.

'I promise,' he kissed her on the forehead and made for the door. By the time he was gone, Rachel already knew what she had to do.

Picking her coat up and leaving just after him,

Rachel waited for the unknown man to leave in his car and then ran to hers, which was parked right next to it.

She had to find out once and for all. If it was something so terrible that even she couldn't be told,

then she'd just have to follow him and see what he was getting up to herself.

Less than ten minutes after departing, they both reached their destination. A couple of cars had pulled out in front of her but she kept her boyfriend's Vauxhall in clear view up front. By the time she pulled up behind him he had already vacated the vehicle. She turned the engine off and took in the surroundings.

She had come to a dead end of an old industrial estate and a desolate warehouse stood in the bleak night. She summoned up enough courage to get out of the car but inside she was frightened.

155

He hadn't been called into work. If he had been lured here maybe he was in terrible danger? She shivered in the cool night and listened carefully for any noise in the area.

After a brief period of time she heard some men talking in the bleak warehouse and decided to go inside.

*

Cold frightened yet determined to find out what her beloved was getting up to, she sneaked into the warehouse, dodging the broken bottles that scattered the path towards it.

Shaking, she kept quiet as she negotiated the already half-open door. With every step she took the voices grew closer. She could make out two voices: one distressed the other cold and mechanical. Surely that couldn't be him. Rachel noticed the two men in an office and crouched down behind a desk at the door and watched the two silhouetted figures continue their engagement.

'But it's impossible. How can you know it was me?'

The distressed voice sounded South African, thought Rachel.

'Because it has your name written all over it. A convicted rapist and swindler who cons rich single women and then kills them. In this case, two hundred thousand pounds goes missing and three women who work for the Private Sector were found strangled with piano wire in their homes. It stinks of you Pietersen.'

'Listen to me, what gives you the right?'

'The police have tried to catch you before. You have dangerous friends in high places – we can't let you go running back to them now, can we? We thought setting up a bogus deal here would trap you and you, my friend, have walked straight into it.'

Rachel could not believe her eyes as she watched her boyfriend produce a pen knife from his pocket.

'No, you can't do this,' the little man pleaded, his figure contorting in terror. Rachel looked on helpless.

'Try and stop me,' the unknown man retorted as he grabbed Pietersen by his shoulders. Pietersen tried to kick and scream himself free but his captor's strength was too much.

With one swoop of the knife he slit the accused man's throat and the blood spurted in the shadows. Rachel had to stuff her coat in her mouth. She felt sick and terrified by what she was watching.

The unknown man let the man's weak body fall to the ground and decided to let him bleed to death. At that point, he realised he was not alone.

'Rachel?'

The love of his life had just seen him commit his first murder. She stood up from her hiding place, about ten metres away from the action, but he could make out her form in the shadows.

Before he could say anything else, Rachel ran as fast she could out of the warehouse and to her car. She screamed as she dropped her car keys, scrambling to get away from this nightmare. She pulled the car door open and drove away as fast as she could, just as her murderer boyfriend ran into view out of the warehouse.

Tears cascaded down her face and she sobbed uncontrollably as she drove back to the flat.

Her drive home was full of the horror of what she had witnessed and her driving very nearly caused an accident with a bus. When she finally got home, she hastily locked the doors and rummaged under the bed for her suitcase. She had to leave before he came back. Her mind was racing with confusion.

She had trusted this man with her life and known him for a good long while and never knew him to be capable of murder. She bundled her clothes into the big suitcase, wiping the tears and snot from her face.

Just as she fastened the suitcase down, a knock at the door made her jump out of her skin.

'Rachel? Rachel, open this door, we have to talk.'

'Go away!' she hollered' I don't want anything to do with you. I'm calling the police.

'Don't do that, they already know. Look, if you would just let me in then I can explain.'

'I'm not letting you back in here. I saw what you did, you fucking murderer! How could you do that?'

'I can't tell you out here. Rachel, I know you are scared but I have to talk to you. I love you and I'd never hurt you. Let me in, please,' the unknown man spoke in a calm tone.

Rachel picked herself up and edged her way to the kitchen. If she were to let him in, she would have to defend herself.

The front door opened and the unknown man saw Rachel, her eyes bleeding mascara and a look of fear contorted on her beautiful face.

'I'm warning you, you can say what you have to say and then I am turning you over.'

He saw the kitchen knife in her hand and held his hands up.

'Okay.'

Slowly she receded back into the shadows on the hallway and he entered the house. They sat down, him on one side of the living room and her on another, still clutching the big knife.

He explained to her calmly the job offer their superior had given him and the ultimatum that came with it.

He had been told not to tell her while he was training just in case it didn't work out and he had to find another job, especially given the nature of it.

She listened to his every word. His explanations for his late nights at work, the struggles he had been having with his conscience and the guilt of having to keep it all a secret from her.

'You know what kind of business we are really in hun, you know that some of the things we are asked to do can be above the board, as it were, and I have felt so bad for keeping it from you until now.'

'Were you really going to tell me when you got back?'

'Yes. I know it has been a shock and I never wanted to get involved in it.'

'How did it feel?' interrupted Rachel.

'I'm sorry?'

'How did it feel? To kill a man. Tell me right now, how did you feel?'

The unknown man sighed. 'Not good. I just switch off, I just feel…numb.'

'And have you done this before?'

'No, tonight was the first time. I'm so sorry.'

Rachel leaned forward and spoke through her teeth.

160

'Don't you dare tell me that you are sorry, stop saying it, you're breaking my heart.'

The statement made him hang his head in shame.

Rachel began to fight back the tears again.

'I wanted to start a family with you. I wanted us to settle down into normal lives and get out of that company as soon as we could. I have found it so hard to talk to you recently but I wanted us to move forward together.'

The unknown man looked her in the eyes and smiled reassuringly.

'We can still do those things.'

'How? You can't have a family if you're an assassin. How would you feel one morning if I had been murdered and our children had been killed too, could you live with yourself? To have the guilt that what you had become had endangered the lives of those you loved the most? You must hate the skin you are in right now.'

The unknown man began to feel tears in his eyes.

'Quit.'

'What?'

'I said quit, run away. Stop while you can and we can start again somewhere. I don't want you to be a murderer,'

'Darling, I can't.'

Rachel began to plead, crying over and over again,

161

'You can! You can!'

The unknown man took hold of her shoulders as she began to get hysterical. She dropped the knife as he touched her, his once warm, safe, comforting embrace now felt cold and unfriendly.

It was dangerous to look into his eyes. He had changed.

'Rachel, listen to me. I have signed the Official Secrets Act. I can't get out. I'm trapped, but I don't want to lose you. Please, don't leave me. I can make you happy and keep you safe. We can get married and have children. Isn't that what you said you wanted?'

Rachel looked up at him and gave him a look that would haunt him for the rest of his life.

'Not from a killer.'

She got up and walked to the bedroom. The unknown man stayed in his position, broken by the events of the night. She reappeared a couple of minutes later wearing her long brown coat and carrying her suitcase.

Exhausted by her emotions she looked down at her love, but not at him. He stayed still.

'I'm going to resign and get out of this city. I'll go stay with relatives for as long as they will have me.

Don't come looking for me otherwise I'll call the police,' she whispered.

Rachel caressed her key to the apartment in her free hand and after a moment's hesitation she put it on the tableside. Without a goodbye, she struggled out of the flat and out of his life forever.

In just one night the unknown man's life had changed dramatically. He had signed his persona away; his name was no longer allowed to be common knowledge.

He had taken his first life and been spied on by his own girlfriend, who then walked out on him.

Something happened to the unknown man that night.

He got up and watched from the living room window as Rachel closed her boot and got in her car. She looked up and saw him looking at her from the living room window, but she did not wave. The engine coughed into life and she drove away.

He never saw her again. As he watched he began to cry uncontrollably and curled up in a ball on the floor.

From that moment on, the unknown man became the unemotional machine he was today.

The cold, calculating killer.

The man who can bring down a whole empire with one squeeze of the trigger.

And all it took was a broken heart.

THE MAN IN THE CORNER

*

RING RING... RING RING

The unknown man was startled from his visions by the abrupt sound of his telephone.

Only one man would call me at this time, what does he want? He wondered, wiping the tears from his eyes.

He got up, pulled the needle from the record yet leaving the needle spinning and picked up the receiver.

'Hello?'

'I have some good news and some bad news.'

The man on the other end did not even have to utter his name. The unknown man knew it was his superior and stood to attention, shaking the melancholy from his body before straightening his back.

'It can't wait until morning so I'm sorry if I woke you.'

'Not at all, what's the matter?'

I have received a message from the Big Chief himself. It arrived around an hour ago and I got here as soon as I could. It's the Big Chief, he wants to meet you.'

'Meet me? You cannot be serious?'

'I'm always serious son, and don't you forget it,' he barked down the line. 'He wants you to meet him at

Elingthorpe Manor in Wales tomorrow. This is the moment we have been waiting for. We know that he will probably be waiting for us but we have a plan to take him down for good. Our years of work look like they will finally pay off. The plan is to send you ahead first and then if things get messy you give us the signal and we go in for him. We shall take no prisoners. This is our moment and we will succeed.'

'And it's definitely him?'

'Definitely. He has even signed it. We've already had it matched with some documents we have kept.'

The unknown man smiled to himself. The Big Chief had been foolish to give away his position. This was to be his chance to wipe out the kingpin for good. He had worked so hard for this moment for so long and now he could retire a happy man if he succeeded in this, his last mission.

'You did say bad news, sir, what can that be?'

The superior's voice took a more solemn tone. 'Ah yes, a few nights ago one of our secretaries had been found sniffing around where she shouldn't have been. It turns out that she is the last spy, the one I had been struggling to find. It was difficult to get information out of her first but in the end she gave in. Turns out she had been looking through your file.

We checked her person, it wasn't on her. We checked our records library, it wasn't there either. We turned over her office, checked her locker, everything. It looks like she had left it for someone to collect who somehow broke in and they got to it before we did.'

'It's a good thing my real name isn't on file anymore otherwise I'd be a dead man then,' said the unknown man.

'Yes…but other information was still on there.'

The unknown man froze in horror.

'What?'

'I'm so sorry son. They have her.'

His pupils dilated in terror. Not Rachel?

'Is she dead?'

'No, but she went missing a couple of days ago. It looks like the Big Chief is holding her at ransom.

This is why he wants to meet you. I don't have to remind you to keep personal feelings out of the picture here. Whatever evil plans he has for her can wait. Do I make myself clear?'

The unknown man was shocked. He slumped back into his chair, his paralysed with the shock.

'Crystal, sir.'

'Good, now if you can make your way over here as soon as possible we shall run through the plan with the others. I may be able to get Sir Michael's help on this. Be here in thirty minutes.'

The line went dead. The Big Chief held the cards. The unknown man put the phone down, the buzz from the dead line failing to shake him out of his daze.

That murderous bastard has Rachel; maybe it was already too late? Maybe he had already killed her? The idea filled him with dread. It was the perfect revenge dish served with a chilling notion. He couldn't bear to think of all the terrible things he was doing to the one woman he ever truly loved.

His aim was clear. He had to save her and kill the Big Chief. Then maybe it could patch things up between them. He knew she hadn't married in the years they had been apart and that he still loved her.

Even if he was barely recognisable from the man she had known a decade earlier, he had to save her life and his own. Repair the damage, if there was anything to salvage.

The unknown man got up out of his armchair like a shot and went over to a side table drawer. Inside there was a handgun and a holster. He picked the holster up and put it around his shoulders, then picked up the gun and housed it in its holder. Before he shut the drawer, he picked up a photograph of Rachel, as he had known her.

It sat in the drawer next to her old key to the flat.

Sweet, kind and beautiful Rachel.

He knew that tomorrow would be a life changer.

'I'm coming for you my love. Nothing else matters.'

CHAPTER TEN

THE BIG CHIEF

It was the beginning of the end. The unknown man knew that. What ever happened in the next few hours, his life would never be the same again. That was if he got out alive.

Every fibre of his being riled against him and his body was tense with the uncertainty in his mind. Ever since he had received the call beckoning him to face his nemesis he hadn't been able to keep his head straight. Even though his superior was confident that this was the moment they had been hoping for, the assassin was more than sceptical.

Why would the Big Chief leave himself so open by giving away his location? It had to be a trap and he was walking straight into the sights of the devil himself. The man who had been responsible for over a quarter of a century of fear and violence, a man who had somehow stayed on top of the pile yet under the radar had seemingly given in.

Or maybe he had a more diabolical plan. And when his superior confirmed the bad news, the unknown man knew that this was no ordinary arrest.

Rachel Smith − the only girl he had ever loved, the one who watched him murder his first victim in cold blood and fled his violent life forever − had been abducted by the Big Chief and was being held hostage at the location. The man was a psychological genius.

He had taken a bite at the unknown man's Achilles heel and it hurt him more than anything else ever could. He shuddered to think what he had done to her.

But if his plan worked, then maybe, just maybe, he could save her too. His superior had told him not to get personal. How could he possibly *not* let this become personal? They had their plan and he secretly had his.

Now the stage was set and a mist descended over the gate he stood outside. Here he was, alone, cold as the rain pelted his body from the furious sky above. He looked through the grill towards the manor house. Elingthorpe Manor stood beyond the gates and seeped through the mist.

The unknown man sighed as he glanced at his wristwatch. Two hours. That's all the time he needed to do it. Refusing to tear his stare away from the exquisite manor, he felt for the intercom button and pressed it hard. As he withdrew his finger, the intercom cracked into life.

'Who is it?' said the male voice at the other end.

'It's me.'

The box went dead. There was no sound, no reply emitting from it. A few seconds passed.

The unknown man could feel his nerves begin to spike through his tense exterior. Then without warning, the old gates began to recede. The metal screeched its way back to allow the figure in.

Breathing deeply, the unknown man made his way up the long gravel path to the front door, where his destiny awaited him.

Several pairs of sneering eyes watched his journey along the sodden gravel path in quiet observation. They were watching through the windows in the old manor and the unknown man could feel their stares burning down upon him.

The way some of the goons had heard the Big Chief talk about him made this man seem like a superman. A legend who walked in the shadows and had the power over life and death at the simple squeeze of his trigger. But there he was: a normal everyday looking man who was walking to − what they had planned would be − his demise.

171

The unknown man finally came to the heavy front door and knocked on it with the big iron hoop that rasped on the old oak. He looked around again; the Big Chief must be feeling confident, he thought to himself, since there were no armed guards waiting for him. He knew he was being watched and he didn't like it. He wasn't used to being observed. This was definitely out of his comfort zone. The door snapped open and three men in navy blue suits greeted him in the doorway, armed with automatic machine guns.

'Get in,' said the one in the middle. Slowly, the unknown man entered the manor. He was now a captured man.

After a vigorous frisking in which his handgun was confiscated, the unknown man was lead to a grand hall.

As he walked along the endless corridors escorted by his three blue-suited minders he glanced at the classic artwork that hung proudly on the walls. He thought to himself what kind of a person he was about to meet.

The most diabolical criminal the country had ever heard of yet never seen. He had many questions he wanted to ask him. No doubt that was exactly the Big Chief wanted to do with him too.

The brisk walk came to end when they stood in the magnificent hall. The unknown man took in his surroundings

172

and was certainly impressed by the splendour, which made him feel slightly sick at himself.

How dare he let himself be seduced by the riches of a megalomaniac? His composure returning, he looked up at the balcony that loomed over the spacious room. As he glared upwards the Big Chief, accompanied by five men who wore the same blue uniform as the three men at the front door, appeared on the balcony like a fake monarch.

'At last we meet; I have been looking forward to this for a long time. Please, take a seat.' The Big Chief beckoned towards two armchairs that sat in a cosy location by the huge fireplace.

Both of the guards either side of the unknown man nudged him in the direction in an aggressive manner.

'No. Be gentle with him. We don't want to harm our guest now do we?'

The unknown man brushed the pleasant gesture aside. As he went over towards one of the armchairs he told himself that he would not be taken in by the kind manners of his enemy.

This man was scum and he wanted to keep the pleasantries down to a minimum.

The Big Chief slipped down the stairs from the balcony towards the other chair. The guards took up their positions all around the room.

'Mind if I join you?' the Big Chief said as the unknown man stared at him, looking straight into his eyes.

Nobody had ever looked at him like that before and lived to tell the tale.

He dissected his features: a mop of white hair, a growing midriff and puffy cheeks from a life of easy living. He was somewhat shocked by what he saw. The man didn't look like a man who could have committed all the crimes that had been caused by him.

'I hope my men don't startle you; what do you think to the house? Pretty spacious isn't it? For a man of my age it helps to keep yourself in comfy surroundings.'

The unknown man remained silent.

'I take it that you are probably wondering why I called you here?'

The Big Chief waited for a response. There was none.

It was as if the young man sitting opposite him was a waxwork. He hadn't moved and he had barely blinked since he had entered the room.

'Well? Have you lost your tongue or something kid?'

The unknown man nodded slowly. He crossed his leg over the other and brought hands up towards his face. Resting his elbows on his knee, the two sets of fingers met and then he continued to stare, intent on not giving anything away.

Not one body movement that would give away the level of hate and anger that was presently flowing through his system.

'Fine,' the Big Chief conceded. 'If you're going to be so difficult to talk to then I'll leave you to my men; I can't stand stubborn young upstarts who think they are the big cock in town. It's your choice.'

The unknown man licked his lips and uttered his first words to his enemy. He so desperately wanted to ask what he had done to Rachel, but then he remembered his superior's famous last words. Don't let it get personal.

'Why did you call for me?'

The Big Chief smiled to such an extent the unknown man thought he was in conversation with the cheshire cat from *Alice in Wonderland*. One thing he knew for sure. This man was just as mad as the fictional character.

'Finally, he speaks!' he shouted, letting the words echo around the grand hall before continuing.

'Why you? Isn't it easy to work out?'

The unknown man shook his head. 'No. A trap perhaps?'

The Big Chief laughed. 'Why on earth would I want to trap you?'

'Because I am the man who is bringing your empire down. I am the one who watches you when you sleep, watches every mistake you make, the voice in the back in your head that whispers whenever you walk alone in a dark place. The nightmare in your dreams. I am the one who will end the pain this nation has endured.'

'Oh are you now? You're a brave one aren't you? You're in the lion's den, my boy, and you are the Christian. Those are big words for such a helpless individual. You have no one here to help you. It's funny really. If your superior hadn't got to you first you would be *my* protégée instead of his. I would have snapped you up as soon as you had made your first kill. We would have been great partners.'

The unknown man scoffed at the claim. 'I don't think so. I have a sense of moral justice and I don't think you could have stomached it.'

'But don't you see son? I'm looking at you now and you are looking at me. Different men yes, but the reflection is the same. We are the same.'

'Never.'

'We have both killed to get where we are. How does it feel? When you are hiding in the dark and pointing a gun at a man's head. Oh, tell me how it feels?'

The Big Chief's taunting was beginning to grate.

'Stop it.'

'Why should I? I want to play with you for a while; you have been a thorn in my side for a long time. That deal between The

Boss and GEMINI was a great loss to me. With that deal I would have controlled the city. Everybody and everything under my guidance.'

'It was my privilege to stop you. I'd do it again any day of the week.'

The Big Chief ignored the attempt to undermine him. He got up out of his chair and went over to the drinks cabinet.

'And then there was Black Diamond,' he continued. 'My best man. I had worked with him for so many years. Within one night he was gone. Still, maybe you did me a favour there. He was drunk on power. He was convinced the deal to cripple the police force would go through, but I never told him that it was only an exercise to overthrow Sir Michael. God, that stupid old fart. I want power son, but even we kings at the top need to take a step back once in a while. I didn't want to be too greedy. As for a trap, no, not a trap — I had to meet you. Hell, I've even risked my own future by inviting you here; I take it your boss knows you are here too? He read my letter? Well it's a good thing that this house is stacked to the rafters with my trained gunfighters then. Trust me, we are well prepared if you want things to turn nasty.'

He made himself a drink, yet ignored the unknown man by pouring only one glass.

Craning his neck for a closer look, the guest noticed his shun.

177

'No drink for me? That isn't the way to treat your guests.'

'Why would I pour you one? You'd only believe that I was trying to poison you.'

He had a point. The unknown man began to ask the questions that had been burning in his mind for quite some time.

'How did you manage to go under the radar for so long? It's clear that the majority of terrorism and other crimes in Great Britain over the last quarter of a century have led right to your door.'

Sitting down with a port in his right hand, the Big Chief began to reminisce.

'Ah, the old days. I was just a simple man. I was privy to all the best financiers in the country. No names, just memories, okay kid? Anyway, we were all in trouble when the Great Recession hit us. We were all about to lose our jobs when I had a brainwave. What if I started a company that distributed parachute payments to companies who were struggling to stay afloat amongst the stormy waves? So, with the last of my money that I had saved up, I set up the business and very soon, using my contacts, I was attached to two dozen of the biggest companies in the country. The deal was that if they met the back payments on the money I loaned them, they would keep going just fine. But if you know your history well, young man,

you will know that many crumbled. That's what happened to many of mine. They couldn't earn enough
to pay me back. So the other half of the deal was, if they couldn't meet the payments, I would take them over and make them mine.'

The unknown man listened to every syllable and it turned over in his head. It was brilliant.

This man knew the right people, had the money and a plan that seemed innocent at first but obviously became consumed by the evil in the mind of the overseer. As he listened further, the Big Chief continued.

'It didn't take long before I was even buying out the major shareholders of just about everywhere. I owned more companies than you have had hot dinners. Big ones, private ones. Pretty soon the scum of the big city crawled out of the woodwork and wanted my help. So they got it, but I now employed *them*. That is how your friend, The Boss, came to my attention. He worked as a worm in other companies and came back to me with the information. I soon punished those who were threatening to dispose of me. So you could say that my supremacy was my goal.'

'But didn't anybody recognize you? How on earth did you stay away from the police?'

'It wasn't too difficult. Golden handshakes with MPs and those alike. They don't like it when their dirty laundry is aired in the open. The list of Members of Parliament I sold to the press and watched them torn to shreds. After a while they learned to keep their mouths shut. First of all, I had never used my own name. That's a little trick I bet even you have been taught isn't it? Well, I bought dwellings around the world and kept myself to myself. I only come home whenever something serious is occurring. The deal that the boss was conducting with GEMINI would have clinched the penultimate cooperation for me. You don't know how comfortable Jamaica is at this time of the year. So here I am. Under the radar, on top of the world.'

'There is no doubt that you are a very clever man, but you have made one big mistake.'

'And what's that then?' the Big Chief enquired.

'Coming back, you have given yourself away.'

The Big Chief got up from his seat and paced the hall.

'While you are here my young man, you can't hurt me. You know that; I know that.'

The unknown man decided to conceal his hand. Help would be here soon.

'Besides, when I show you who I have waiting for you, you will have no choice but to obey me.'

180

The unknown man's eyes grew wild with anger. His plan to hide his feelings was slipping fast.

'Oh there it is,' the Big Chief mocked. 'The look of a killer.'

'Where is she?' the unknown man demanded.

'You know who it is obviously. It's a shame isn't it? How a job can come between young love?'

The unknown man's face contorted with anger. 'What have you done to her?'

The Big Chief's eyes met his enemy's and he stared threateningly into them.

'I was about to ask you the same question.'

The unknown man glared back. He knew what his nemesis was talking about, how he had broken her heart all those years ago.

'Would you like to see her?'

'I swear that if you have harmed so much as a hair on her head I will make you pay.'

The Big Chief ignored the emotional retort and stared at the man who was gripping hard to the arms of the chair.

'Remember your surroundings. I can crush you just as quickly as you can open your mouth and talk.'

He looked up and indicated the row of blue-suited soldiers on the balcony. The unknown man looked up also. He had to

181

be careful. If his plan were to go ahead with no hiccups he would have to play ball and bite his lip. Hard.

'Take me to her.'

After being led by two armed men down a long corridor in the manor, the unknown man was beginning to feel very nervous. He had not seen Rachel in years and the last time he had seen her, both they're hearts were broken. He had rehearsed what he was going to say but none of that mattered now.

In a few moments they were going to be reunited, and he was going to save her, whether she like it or not.

The walk ended when the unknown man and his entourage came to a dark coven where they lay a heavy wooden door. It was bolted from the outside and one of the guards went to unbolt it. The other turned to his prisoner.

'We'll be outside, don't do anything funny now or we'll have you.'

The unknown man shook his head and took a deep breath, then went inside. There, sitting on the bed with a petrified look across her face, Rachel looked up into the eyes she hadn't looked into for so long.

'You!'

Rachel hadn't changed. Sure she was older, but in the unknown man's eyes she had only became more beautiful with age. Yet the look of fear was still fixed on her face.

His eyes were different − they were cold and unwelcoming. It wasn't the same man she had fallen in love with.

'Are you alright?' He went over to the bed to sit with her.

'Stay away!' She demanded.

The unknown man recoiled and turned to the guards who were watching in the doorway.

'Could you give us a few minutes please? Come on, I'm not going anywhere am I? Just a few minutes!'

The guards looked at each other and closed the door, bolting it so that he was now trapped with Rachel.

The unknown man turned back to her. She had moved up to the head of the bed.

'Have they harmed you in any way?'

'No, no, they haven't. Stay back.'

Rachel still hadn't forgiven him for what he had done the night they had separated. In her eyes he was a killer. Coupled with the shock of being held hostage and then the man she was most scared of in the entire world entering her prison, she felt scared for her safety.

Within a few moments, the steely glaze that was fixed in his eyes had melted away and she saw the man she had once loved

183

once again. It was as if somebody had turned a switch on inside him and he had reverted to the caring man he had once been.

'I'm not going to harm you Rachel, I never could. Please find it in your heart to trust me, just this once.'

He sat down on the other side of the bed and held his hand out to her. Tentatively, she held hers out too and they held hands. They were one once more.

'How long have you been here?'

'A couple of days. They took me from my home. They tied me up and put me in the boot of their car. I thought it had something to do with you. That's why you're here isn't it? They are holding me hostage to get to you?'

He nodded. 'I'm afraid so, they stole some old records and found you that way.'

'Because they know that you still have feelings for me?'

Rachel snapped her hand away and got up from the bed.

'I knew it. This is why I couldn't stay with you. I knew that one day the job would endanger my life as much as yours. How could you?'

'Rachel, I know that you are mad, but please listen to me. I have come to rescue you.'

'How? You're not armed, surely?'

'No, they took my gun away. But that doesn't matter. We just have to play for time.'

'For time? Why?'

The unknown man smiled for the first time in a long while.

'You'll see. I can't tell you in case the guards are listening in but help is on its way. The Big Chief has bitten off more than he can chew this time.'

Rachel looked at him and snorted.

'And you think that I will want to come with you? Dream on, Mister.'

'Rachel, please. I'm not trying to prove myself to you. I just want you safe.'

Rachel sat down by her former lover and looked him in the eyes.

'So you still work for the Service then?'

He looked down evading her gaze. 'Yes, but not for much longer. I've grown tired Rachel; this isn't the life I want. Not anymore. All I want is for the Big Chief to be stopped. That's all I have wanted for a long time. Apart from…'

'Yes?' she interrupted.

'Apart from you, that is. I made a mistake, Rachel, and when we get out of here and you can find it in your heart to forgive me then that would mean the world to me.'

185

'But you don't know if I'm married, if I have a family. For all you could know, a husband and children are at home worrying about me right now.'

The unknown man edged closer to her.

'I know that isn't the case. Just trust me on this. Please.'

Rachel looked longingly into his eyes and finally gave in. She nodded, tears in her eyes and threw her arms around his neck. They embraced for what seemed like an eternity. The unknown man squinted hard, holding back the tears and smelt her hair in his face. The she whispered something that melted his heart.

'I missed you.'

Their reunion was interrupted by the sound of a helicopter cutting through the storm clouds outside. Pulling away from the embrace, the unknown man got up from the bed and looked out of the window and watched as the helicopter disappeared from view and landed outside another part of the manor. He looked to the left and through the rain splattered glass he saw what looked like the distant blue siren lights of police cars bleeding through the steel gates. At the same time, he could hear a commotion occurring in other rooms of the grand manor.

He looked down at his watch and then looked back up at Rachel, who was looking back at him with a curious look on her pretty face. His mouth formed a friendly smile − but the steel determination had returned in his eyes.

'It's started.'

CHAPTER ELEVEN

DUEL TO THE DEATH

The black helicopter tore through the grey clouds like a wire through flesh. The unwelcoming din of noise that it produced whirled through the air like the propeller that took it to its destination. Inside, a heavily armed unit of men sat patiently waiting for the moment they would be called into action. The men, sitting side-by-side and opposite one another in two cramped rows, had been well trained and barely flinched in the uncomfortable surroundings.

Years upon years of gruelling effort and the endless drills they had endured had transformed the young men into expert soldiers. They had been briefed only an hour before at their barracks by their commanding officer, who sat at the end of one row with a white beret, while his officers wore red ones. He had told them their mission – to take down the inhabitants of the manor and capture their main target alive. They were not the only ones.

As the party of a three-dozen soldiers leaned to the side, the helicopter was fast approaching the end of its journey. The noise level inside the helicopter was deafening but they could all still hear their superior barking the final orders over the sound of the propeller chopping through the strong wind and rain.

'Right lads, we're nearly there,' yelled the Commander, whose voice was hoarse. The soldiers readied their automatic machine guns in unison, as if they were all operated by the same puppeteer.

'Remember the plan,' the Commander continued. 'Take down the resistance and bring out the Big Chief alive, Operation Foxtrot commences as soon as we land. Keep low. We will be landing in the grounds and they'll be hearing us coming. Remember,' he hollered.

'I want the Big Chief reprimanded not killed. Bring him to me alive!'

As the helicopter whirled its way towards Elingthorpe Manor, down below, a black BMW, escorted by four police cars with their blue lights and wailing sirens blaring, was also heading for the same destination.

Inside, Sir Michael Houghton, the man who had so very nearly fallen to the Big Chief's might, was accompanied by another important part of Operation Foxtrot. The Head of the Secret Service stared over his shoulder and sat opposite his old friend. As he looked out of the back window, the superior went over the plans in his head.

It had been a quiet journey, but the anticipation and hope that they would finally have their man was beginning to build inside him.

'Not long now,' assured Sir Michael, who had to shout over the noise of the sirens. He had arranged for the local roads to be evacuated and for roadblocks to stop any traffic from blocking the route. What would have been an hour and a half journey on a regular day had turned into a forty-five minute dash. Both men had watched as their car sped along the streets.

The motorway had been fine yet rather dull, yet as they came to more built up areas, they could see the blur of people on the street pavements looking quizzically at their entourage.

One young boy had even waved at the car and the superior had leaned forward to give a wave back through the back window, which Sir Michael had found rather absurd.

Still, they were nearly at their destination and the trap was very nearly complete.

'So, does you're man know what time the plan will be going into operation?'

'Yes he knows,' the superior's still voice was louder than it normally was but its tone hadn't changed. He meant business, even if he did occasionally wave to the passers-by like a monarch.

'If he is set to the same clock as us then he should have been there a couple of hours ago. Hopefully he is still there now and the Big Chief is none the wiser to what is going to happen.'

'By the sounds of it this Big Chief character sounds like an intelligent sort of fellow. I think he may suspect what is about to happen. You can't go about giving your location away to the people who are hunting you in the first place. No my friend, I am preparing for war.'

As the car entered Elingthorpe the rain began to tear down like they were entering a drive-through car wash.

'I think someone must have told the weatherman what we are about to do,' quipped the superior.

He continued to look out of the window and returned to his thoughts. As they arrived outside the big iron gates of the manor, he thought of how his man inside was doing.

The unknown man had been watching the descent all along. During his reunion with Rachel, he had been aware that the time had nearly come. Now it was his turn to spring into action.

'We're going to have to act fast if we want to get out alive,' he said as his face returned to its more serious look.

'What you mean? This is an ambush?' Rachel sat on the bed and began to fear for her life again.

'Yes, but we're not involved.'

'What do you mean?' Rachel was rather taken back by what she took to be a silly answer.

'How can we possibly not be involved? We're trapped my darling. I was kidnapped and you are part of this. One way or another we're involved that's for sure, or had you forgotten that?'

The unknown man had no time for sarcasm.

'Whatever happens now, stay close to me. It's my job to get you out safely, not to bring you into battle. You're a civilian. Therefore, it is their responsibility to capture the Big Chief and mine is to keep you safe.'

'But how are we going to get out? There are two men with guns outside and we don't have anything to defend ourselves.'

'I have already thought of that. Any moment now they are going to tear in here and take us prisoner again.'

He grabbed her by the hand and pulled her up onto her feet. Picking up a heavy candle stand, he forced it into her hand. She knew what he was asking of her.

'No, darling I can't,' she insisted.

'Look, I hate to ask this of you, but we have to get out. I swear that as soon as we get out of here I will never ask anything like this of you again. Trust me.'

At that moment they heard the heavy wooden door creak into life. The unknown man forced Rachel behind the door and he stood the other side. She began to shake.

She had no idea if she had the strength of character to do this. Still, she'd give it a go if it meant that they were going to escape alive, even if it meant injuring another human being. Was this the thought that crossed her ex-boyfriend's mind every time he was assigned a mission? Who wanted that on their mind?

The wooden door crashed open and one of the guards rushed in the room. The sudden nature of his arrival made Rachel jump and it was this impulse that had told her body to force the heavy object down onto the top of his head.

The unknown man watched as the stricken guard winced in pain and collapsed on the floor. In the blink of an eye he dropped to the floor, just as the other guard readied his gun. Rachel sheltered behind the door, dropping the candle stand from her grasp and fell into a ball.

She heard a gunshot fired and screamed. She closed her eyes, fearing the worst. A few moments later, the victor of the short fight pulled the door back and looked down on her cowering figure. It was her lost love, with the guard's gun in his hand.

'How did you do that?'

The unknown man smiled. 'Grabbed your friend's gun and got the other before he had a chance to fire. Come on. We have to move fast.'

He grabbed her hand and pulled her to her feet. He had already taken the ammunition from the dead man on the floor and found another pistol on his person.

Not looking back, the couple left the room.

They knew they now had a fight on their hands.

In the main hall, the Big Chief sat back in his luxurious chair with his eyes closed and his hands closed together with his index fingers meeting, tapping his lips.

He had heard the helicopter landing, the police sirens outside and the gunfire upstairs. Yet he was in deep thought. He knew this would happen and he was well prepared. He heard shouting from both outside and inside and felt the ever-approaching footsteps of one of his soldiers pound towards him.

'Sir, we've been ambushed.'

The Big Chief said nothing, still deep in his thoughts.

'Sir?'

The Big Chief opened his eyes.

'Defend the manor. Get me the man and the girl.'

The soldier nodded and rasped the orders along the hall to the blue-attired guards who awaited instructions.

At the same time the Big Chief, whose trance like state was broken, leapt up out of his chair and paced towards one of the grand cabinets.

Rummaging in the drawers, he picked up a pistol. If nothing else, he was going to bring down the man who had instigated his downfall.

Meanwhile, outside in the pouring rain, the soldiers were being deployed. The helicopter gave them brief cover from any aggressive fire they may come under but it soon took to the skies once again, leaving the small force taking shelter behind the walls separating the garden and the vast hall. There, they waited.

'Okay, this is your one and only chance.' The superior stood outside the gates alongside the police and Sir Michael, issuing orders from a megaphone.

'We will not show aggression if you turn yourself over. If you show us any malice we will retaliate. If you come quietly with your hands up, there will be no need for action. If you don't we will force our way in. It's your choice.'

The superior removed the megaphone from his lips and waited. It seemed like an age and the silence was eerie. There was no movement from within the manor and everyone present was beginning to feel edgy. The sodden air was rank with tension.

'Right, move! I...'

The superior's order was interrupted by the sound of a gunshot through glass. The shot had come from one of the higher rooms in the Manor. Soon, the fire was retaliated on and a gunfight ensued.

'Binoculars, quick!'

The superior became a little anxious. The Big Chief was smart. He had been waiting for them all along. He had placed gunmen on the roof, in the rooms on the top floor and even on the ground floor. The battle had begun.

The unknown man and Rachel ran along the corridors, stopping every time they saw one of the Chief's guards. Luckily for them, the majority of them were sitting at the windows, some open, some closed, and the sound of bullets hailed through the Manor.

It echoed a sound of death that penetrated the couple's senses. He looked over to Rachel occasionally as they ran. She was white with fear and her pupils had dilated. She was

197

terrified and he had to protect her. It was his mission to do so, even if it were a personal one.

He still had another job to do too. In one hand, the unknown man held the gun he had acquired from the guards at the bedroom door. Every now and again, if the room that the gunshots were coming from was open, he would line both of them up against the wall
and then fire into the room, taking the gunman by surprise. Rachel squeezed her eyes wide shut to blot out the destruction she was witnessing.

'Come on.'

They continued along the corridor, still holding hands and the unknown man occasionally firing on the guards they encountered. They were startled by a gunshot from behind them. One of the guards had caught up with them. The pair dropped to the floor as soon as they heard the bullet whistle through the air. It had kept going and missed both of them by a foot to the right.

The unknown man returned the fire and shot three bullets of hot steel into the guard's chest. The guard recoiled in agony and the spray of blood from his wounds clouded his figure as it fell – defeated – to the ground. The pair picked themselves up and their attention returned to their escape. They would have to pick the pace up now that the Big Chief's men knew they had escaped.

The bullets continued to rain towards the foot soldiers in their makeshift shelters. It was hard for them to see the exact location of the gunmen in the weather they were fighting in.

Their berets sodden with water and their trigger fingers sopping in the damp conditions, they returned their attack at the bedrooms.

Slowly, the soldiers edged their way closer to the manor. They had to get in and bring the Big Chief out alive.

'What's going on in there?'

Sir Michael was beginning to get itchy feet. The sound of the gunfire was irradiating its way outside the manor's gates and reaching those who were opposed by them. The superior was still looking onto the battlefield through his binoculars, like a general directing the battle from a far away location.

He desperately wanted to be involved but they knew that had to wait. They couldn't break their way in and endanger the mission. If Operation Foxtrot were to be a success, they would have to wait until the Big Chief was brought out by the troops. But as the sound of falling rain and metal pierced the dreary atmosphere, he wondered how his agent was getting on.

*

'Stay back!'

Rachel got down and did what she was told. They had come to the end of the corridor and the stairwell was their next obstacle. She looked behind her, the sound of guns drawing ever closer.

'Hurry!' Her shrill command was barely audible over the noise. The unknown man edged over the banister and observed the hall. There were two guards by the main door, shooting out of man-made holes in the glass to keep the assaulting soldiers at bay.

If the Big Chief did indeed own the manor as his secret (until now) English home, he didn't mean for it to be standing for much longer, thought the unknown man.

He had little time to feel sentimental over the antique surroundings though. With a devastating squeeze of his trigger, he wiped the two gunmen out.

Before going back to fetch Rachel he delved into his pocket and changed the magazine. He had been picking up the ammunition of his fallen adversaries along the way.

Now, their escape route was clear. Glancing around the hall one last time, he ran back and leaned down to Rachel's hiding place. He crouched down to her level and kissed her hard on the forehead.

'Nearly there. We just have to go down the stairs and we are free.'

'But won't we be shot at when we are outside?'

'No, not even our men are stupid enough to fire at us. They know the plan. But we will have to run as fast as we can when we get outside. Just in case. Do you think you can do that for me?'

'Of course I bloody can!' He felt the fighting spirit flow through Rachel's blood.

'Good girl,' he smiled. He helped her up onto her feet and put his free arm around her shoulder. Tentatively, they stepped out onto the stairwell.

With a sense of trepidation, they sprinted down the old wooden stairs, each step bringing them closer to freedom. As soon as they stepped off the final step, they both smiled and made for the door.

Just as they stepped over the two corpses on the floor and the unknown man reached for the handle, a familiar voice grabbed their attention.

'Going so soon?'

The unknown man sighed and turned around. Rachel began to shake in fear. Behind them there stood the Big Chief, gun in his hand and flanked by three of his personal guards. The unknown man dropped his gun and gave an apologetic look to his crestfallen lover. Only one thing now seemed certain to him and that was death.

'Fall back!' The order ran around the manor, uttered by more than one of the Big Chief's army. The soldiers had advanced considerably since the start of the showdown.

They had surrounded the manor with only minor injuries. It hadn't helped that they were probably better equipped than the men defending the Big Chief since they had body armour and the men inside hadn't.

The men fell back and took up ranks inside the main hall. They were willing to make a big stand. Another segment went to the main doors, missing the captured couple and the Big Chief leaving the entrance by about a minute. The group positioned by the doors dragged their dead comrades' bodies to one side and took up similar positions.

Outside the doors, the Commander was planning a more than effective way of breaching the stronghold.

He radioed in to Sir Michael for permission to use what he thought would be the best method.

'Red Fox to Silver Sword come in please.'

*

Sir Michael left the party watching the action unfold and returned to the shelter of his personal car. He had overheard his communication device go off because the firing had died down and it was so quiet outside the gates, you could hear a pin drop. The tension was growing and no one dare utter a word in case they missed a crucial moment.

'Silver Sword here, go on Commander.'
The small unit that was connected to his seat buzzed into life again.

'Permission to go in, Sir.'

Sir Michael had little regard for the damage this would do to the ancient manor. It could be salvaged if that is what the Government wanted to do.

'Permission granted. Just get the Chief. Use any force necessary if you have to.'

'Very good, sir,' the communicator buzzed and then fell silent again. At the same time as Sir Michael put the communicator back in its hold, he was startled by the influx of cars that descended on the grounds. He sighed to himself. Journalists. They must have got past the roadblock. Before he had a chance to order the police to keep them back a bang was heard from the grounds.

The army had blasted they're way in. Grenades had worked and wiped out the resistance at the door. They were in the building. But was the king still in his counting house?

The unknown man and Rachel were being held at gunpoint in the kitchen of the war torn manor. At the Big Chief's demand, they were being cuffed to the flue pipe that poked out of the top of the old fashioned cooker.

The kitchen itself was dark and dingy, nothing like the splendour of the décor that spoilt the rest of the grand house. It was small and pokey, dark due to the grey clouds outside blotting out the sunlight, and it was about to be the place where the fight would end. Rachel looked hopelessly at her lover.

Occasionally she sobbed a little but then stifled her fear as best as she could. After the cuffs were secure, the Big Chief, with a gun in his hand, beckoned for the three guards to come nearer.

'Leave us now; keep the resistance at the door, all we can do is play for time. When that time comes meet me at the south side.'

As the three men left the small kitchen, the Big Chief pulled a chair from under the preparation table and sat on it looking at his nemesis.

204

'Play for time? What time? Didn't you feel that tremor? You have lost. Even if you kill us now you won't get out of this alive.'

'Don't play the hero because the little lady is here, son. I have means of an escape. I was prepared for this. You on the other hand, weren't.'

He played with his handgun as if he was toying with the ultimate fate of the couple.

'Now, how can I finish you off? So many choices.'

Rachel's body stiffened. The unknown man remained calm.

The Big Chief got up off the chair and walked over to the set of knives on the table.

'I could make a hole in your guts and watch you bleed to death. I could shoot you right now or I could make it as painful as I can – or I can combine all of the above.'

The unknown man had a plan. But he would have to be quick and crafty if it were to mean the escape of him and his girl. With his bound hand he turned the dial on the cooker, automatically turning the gas on.

'Why do you want to kill both of us? Why drag Rachel into this?'

'Because, you have destroyed me. If I wanted to make you suffer then I should kill her first. Yes. I want to see the look in both your eyes as I jab this knife in her back,' he picked up the biggest butcher knife. 'The look on your face as you watch her die in utter torment. She broke your heart. Do you want me to break it for a second time?'

The unknown man ignored the threat. He began to smell the gas, as did Rachel. Drained by the fear and panic she had endured, she accepted her lover's plans when he gave her a wink with the eye that was facing away from their captor.

'Even if you do kill us, there is nowhere for you to go. We know what you look like now. We know who you are and where your accounts are kept. Your empire has crumbled. You have fallen so far we wouldn't even have to crush you in the dirt.'

The Big Chief raged at the pair, making both of them jump.

'You think you have defeated me? No one can stop me, not even you!'

The gas began to flood the kitchen, yet the Big Chief was so wound up he barely noticed.

Maybe he thought it was fallout from the battle that had occurred outside, the unknown man thought. Any minute soon, they were going to begin coughing and then they would have to make their final move.

'What do you think this is a Bond film? No, I've had enough of this. You'll regret ever trying to sabotage my life. I'm going to kill you first.'

'Think again,' threatened the unknown man. At that moment the Big Chief had come close enough for the unknown man to strike. He had wound him up so well, the Big Chief had played into his plans. With his head only inches away, the unknown man head butted him across the bridge of the nose, sending the Big Chief flying backwards.

As he hit the floor, the unknown man used all his strength to tip the cooker over, breaking the flue and setting them free. Even though the couple were still cuffed together, Rachel suddenly felt her strength return to her being.

'Get the gun!' she screamed.

The unknown man kicked the gun across the kitchen floor and made for the door. The Big Chief, his face bleeding and his eyes as wild as a wolf, grabbed his shoe just as the couple were making for the kitchen door. He dragged them both down to the ground.

Rachel kicked out at the tyrant and caught a few blows herself on her leg. The gas was becoming unbearable. The unknown man punched and jabbed at his greatest enemy, both scrapping like children on the cold stone floor.

207

As they fought, Rachel scrambled for the gun but it was no good. The gun was a few inches out of her reach. She tugged at the handcuffs, trying to create more of a stretch for the weapon. However, she was dragged back into the fight as the Big Chief grabbed the upper hand. He threw his fists down on the unknown man, blow after blow knocking the wind out of the assassin.

All three of them were beginning to cough more violently as the poisonous gas flooded their lungs.

Rachel couldn't bear to think that she may die like this. Summing up all the strength left in her terrified body, she threw a punch so hard it met the Big Chief's already broken nose and lifted him off the lap of the unknown man and onto the floor.

The unknown man looked up at his beautiful ex-lover and smiled. The Big Chief writhed on the floor.

'Are you okay?' Rachel asked. The unknown man couldn't believe it. Here they were choking to death, trying to escape from what had become a battleground and he had just been beaten quite severely and she was asking if he was okay? He didn't care though. He nodded and indicated to the door.

'Come on. We have to get out,' Rachel helped him to his feet and they made for the door. As they opened it they breathed

208

the clean, dank air outside. They had done it. But as they went to step outside, they heard the Big Chief behind them again.

His empire ruined. His last line of defence was about to give in to the superior soldiers who were now in the house and knowing he could never really escape those who hunted him. He picked the gun up off the floor and pointed it at the unknown man. If he squeezed the trigger, with the amount of gas that had now clouded he kitchen and replaced the air with a transparent poison, it would surely kill them all.

'If I can't win then neither can you.'

'No!' The unknown man screamed. 'Rachel, run!'

The Big Chief squeezed the trigger.

*

Back at the gates, the superior had witnessed the soldier's grenade their way past the main door and drive their way into the manor.

As the sound of gunfire spread to the safety of the other side of the gates, an explosion so load drowned the sound of fighting out, knocking him, Sir Michael, the half dozen police force members and the journalists who had arrived to grab a story, to the ground.

KA BOOOOMMMMM!

A fireball surged up through to the roof of the east side of the manor and shone like an Olympic torch, blowing debris of the once great manor across the grounds and decimating the building. A cloud of thick, black smoke whirled high into the raining sky. The grand manor was devastated.

After the sound of the explosion receded and the fire continued to rage, the sound of flames licking the info structure replaced the previous sound of bullets. A still silence hung through the air.

The battle was over.

In the mind of the shell shocked superior who held his head on the puddle-ridden road for cover. All he could think of was the feeling of this being the end of the Big Chief and quite possibly, the unknown man.

CHAPTER TWELVE

THE FINAL END

Dawn was breaking on a new day for the inhabitants of the big city. The gloom of the night was slowly defeated by a wash of red that bled into the skyline. It was as if the light was battling the dark for the supremacy of a clear morning. It was the most beautiful, natural sight that the people who occupied the grey urban landscape could only hope to see, yet most never saw.

As they were still cocooned in their beds, their slumber preventing them the threat of glorious sunshine breaking through the sky, an old man, eyes worn by the horrors he had witnessed but been privy to organising stood alone by a window in the tallest room of a sky scraping tower. Pre-occupied by his thoughts, he watched the sunrise, but was un-impressed by its natural beauty. His melancholic, heavy eyes sank. His mission was complete. His best man was gone.

Even though a few days had passed since the incident, the head of his empire had witnessed firsthand another fall to rubble within an instant. In a matter of seconds, a quarter of a century of planning, man effort and lives lost came to a climax of fire and fallen timber, the result taking the main perpetrator of evil and his best agent.

As he approached his seventieth year on this world, the superior had grown weary of the madness that he had seen.

There had been far too many deaths, too many painful decisions that equated to memories. He sighed and bowed his head, his body silhouetted by the sun flooding into his office. The events of a few days ago were definitely taking their toll.

As the superior closed his eyes, the flashback of the explosion that had ripped through the grand old manor house and knocked those outside flying to the floor replayed in his mind.

The rain poured, the clouds seemed to have sensed the air of tension and were as black as a bad man's heart. The fight had been abrupt, that was the plan.

The armed forces that infiltrated the main hall had fought with the armed personnel that the Big Chief had flanked himself with. In a little over half an hour, as those who were hunting him were still battling their way through the manor, an explosion of such force silenced the sound of gunfire and roared through the storm.

Looking up from his hiding place, the superior stared up and saw a fireball soaring out of the eastern side of the manor,

212

shattering all the windows that once stood firmly in their frames. After what seemed like an eternity, the magnificent red and orange flame died down from its brilliant ball of destruction and licked angrily in the chasm that now stood devastated.

Those around him – including Sir Michael, who had wanted to oversee the siege himself – slowly got to their feet and gaped in horror at the fire.

The flames soon began to spread through the manor and a sea of bodies, from both warring factions, soon stumbled from the entrance they had forced only minutes earlier. Some held their hands to their mouths, spluttering as the black smoke raged in their lungs.

Screams emitted from the engulfed manor and soon the bodies that ran out through the thick smoke were alight themselves. All of a sudden, those who had been sparring with bullets seconds previously were now helping each other to put out the flames that licked around their flesh.

When the emergency services had arrived on the scene, with the press in full tow, some had already succumbed to their injuries and others writhed in pain as the skin burned. The smell was disgusting.

The superior tried to help as best as he could, making sure those who were wounded made their way to an ambulance,

213

desperately avoiding the gaze of the media who had been kept out by the barely functioning iron gates positioned down the long gravel path to the manor.

He was frantically checking the faces of all those who had been caught in the explosion – even the corpses that were laid out and covered by shrouds that now littered the path. He was desperate to find confirmation that they had got their man that the long war was now over. As the rain continued to fall and the fire licked through the carcass of the manor, he watched the fire services try to contain the flames and accepted what thought as the truth. The Big Chief was dead and so was his number one agent.

The girl?

He wasn't sure, maybe that was always a bluff, just to tempt the unknown man to this demise. He bowed his head and walked back towards Sir Michael.

'Any sign of him?'

The superior shook his head despondently.

'It's highly unlikely anybody on that side of the house would have survived the blast.'

'What on earth do you think caused it?'

'I'm not sure at the moment Sir Michael. All I can say is if he was in there, it is now over, after all these years.'

Sir Michael could sense an air of sadness surrounding his old friend. He put his hand on the superior's shoulder and looked down to him and smiled.

'Look, as soon as the fire is out we will begin to investigate thoroughly. We know what the Big Chief looks like now, thanks to intelligence. I'm sure we got him.'

'It's not the Big Chief that concerns me. I sent a man in there. A good man. A man who without his skill and determination we would never have got this far. He went in first and I haven't seen him come out. For the first time in decades Sir Michael, I feel as if I've lost.'

Sir Michael put his arm around the superiors shoulder and led him back towards to the car.

'We haven't lost my friend, we have won. The war is over, it's the end. The final end.'

The superior shook his head as if he were shaking the dust off. He didn't want to start getting too preoccupied by presumptions until there was concrete news.

That's why he had been waiting in the office all night. His weariness and fatigue had made him fight back with several mugs of coffee, and the odd bit of paperwork he had been pushing back that needed finishing had kept him awake.

The boys in the office would have news for him this morning, and he hoped it was good news.

For a man who had been there and done that and was so respected yet feared at the same time, many of his work colleagues would not have forgiven him for being partly responsible for the unknown man's apparent death. Indeed, he had selected the young man himself many years earlier but then came to regret the decision.

Not because he had recruited a terrible assassin but because he had made a broken man. He knew that telling the unknown man to keep his new job secret would be tough and that his former employee Rachel had a relationship with him, which further complicated matters.

Then the night after he had dispatched his new apprentice on his first kill, it was clear that something changed inside the unknown man. Rachel handed in her notice and never returned to work and the once jovial, social young man became a cold, secluded shell from which he had never broken free. As the superior reminisced about those early days with his favourite employee, a timid knock could be heard from the office door.

'Come in.'

It was his secretary, Maria Ferris. She had been by her superior's side for many years and knew the company inside out. She was perhaps the closest he had ever come to a wife, as close as you can get when married to your job. She was in her late fifties, about five foot three and wore a business suit to work. Like her superior she had been up all night too and upon entry to the office, she sighed when she saw how tired her boss looked.

'Still here then?' she asked even though she knew the answer.

'How can I be anywhere else? Any news yet?'
Maria shook her head. The superior huffed and sat back down in his burgundy leather chair.

'Well then, looks like I'll be waiting here a little longer then.'
Maria looked concerned. 'Sir, why don't you go home, get some rest. I can send you a message when we have the news?'

The superior looked up at her and smiled a smile that lacked confidence.

'You're a good girl Maria. No, I'll wait. It's given me a chance to do some work at the very least, I was rather hoping that you'd have gone home by now though?'

'No sir, I'll stay here with you... well, somebody's got to keep you company, eh?'
The superior laughed quietly. Maria was the only person he allowed to speak to him like an equal.

She was very dear to him and he cared for her like a daughter.

'You should have gone home to your husband hours ago.'

'Greg doesn't mind. What seems to be troubling you Sir? I'm sure the news will be good news?'

The superior opened his mouth to begin his next sentence but paused and beckoned his secretary to sit down in a chair opposite his on the other side of the desk. She sat down and smiled.

'Honestly, sir, you haven't been the same over the past few days.'

The superior smiled back and began to confide in her. The only woman he could truly confide in.

'I've had a lot on my mind. Operation Foxtrot. The loss of life, the way the media intercepted the story. It was front page news, Maria. The red tops had a field day when Elingthorpe Manor went up. Double page spreads of the Big Chief's goons and our police burning on the ground. Makes you wonder why people want to read them.'

He picked up his black ink pen and started fiddling with it in his hands.

'You're worried about him, aren't you Sir?'

The superior looked up and the colour washed out of his face like a wave retreats back after crashing on the seabed.

'That boy was supposed to be my heir. I felt like he would take over from me one day. Like I could trust him implicitly. But my methods were all wrong back then, Maria. I made him

218

and helped break him. You should have seen him before his promotion. All smiles and jokes. He used to bring a ray of sunshine into the room. All he did after his first assignment was bring a chill to it. It was as if he had shut down. I did that to him.'

'Of course you didn't, sir. You did what you had to do. Without him we would never have been able to bring the Big Chief down. The country is a safer place thanks to him, and you.'

The superior snorted.

'Maria, at the end of the day, we are nothing but killers. I had a feeling that Operation Foxtrot would be my last job. My final curtain. But over the last few years I have had my suspicions about that boy. He was more machine than man. And what can I retire to? The hunger was waning and I wouldn't want to retire with some of the darker memories in my mind.'
'But as soon as you do, sir, you would regain your life – your identity.'

'There is nothing left of my identity Maria. I am an old man. I have been here since I was a young man making my way up the system to the top. My head is swimming with thoughts. On one hand I don't want the Big Chief to be dead so that I can continue to fight another day. On the other I want that boy to be okay and to come back and relieve me.'

219

'Both may happen, you never know. Just stay positive and for my sake I hope you won't be leaving too soon. I enjoy working for you, Sir.'

The superior got up from his chair and walked back over to the window. He then turned and smiled at Maria.

'That will be all Maria.'

Maria smiled and picked herself up out of her chair and made for the door. After she opened the door she turned back and looked at the old man staring out of the window, his brain working like clockwork.

'I'm sure it will all work out for the best, sir,' she said as she shut the door behind her.

The superior exhaled deeply and continued to look down upon the sun-flooded streets below.

A couple of hours flew by. Newspaper stalls were setting up below him and the postman's red van was easy to spot in the grey spaghetti of roads below. There's an honest job, he thought. He'd be too old for that now though. Maybe he could be a bus driver instead. It's what his Dad did for fifty years. His train of thought was well and truly lost as his secretary came rushing in to the room.

'Sir, sir, I've got a message from one of our agents at the scene of the explosion! Agent Wilshire has just delivered it. It's from Sir Michael himself, must have rung but not been able to get through to us, so he wrote it down and Agent Wilshire has brought it himself.'

The superior gulped. This was the moment he had been waiting for all night long.

'For God's sake Maria, spit it out woman, don't leave me hanging on your words.'

Maria opened the letter and read the contents.

'It reads:

To the Head of Her Majesty's National Interests
Bureau,

Sorry I can't bring you this news myself. There is still quite a bit of work to be done here. It appears that the explosion was caused

by a gas leak that triggered off other small explosions in the east of Elingthorpe Manor. After an extensive investigation we have come to the conclusion that indeed the Big Chief was killed in the initial explosion...'

Maria looked up at her superior who showed no emotion at the news.

'I told you sir, didn't I tell you! It's over. He got him!'

The superior put his finger up to his lips indicating for his excited assistant to keep calm.

'Is there anything else?'

Maria composed herself. 'Yes sir,' she continued.

> *'...The final body count is seventeen. Twelve fatalities on our side and the arrests that were carried out indicate that we did indeed get our man. I must commend you on your team and your own conduct, and the way in which you conducted yourselves to make Operation Foxtrot the success it was. I shall meet you later on today to make our report to the PM. If you want to contact me before then please try ringing me on the attached number. For some reason my personal phone isn't working at this site. I will be in my office from 8am.*
> *Yours,*
> *. Sir Michael Houghton.'*

'That is good news. He is right you know. It is over.'

The superior went to sit back down in his comfortable chair. Tapping his chin with his fingers, he turned to his secretary.

'Okay Maria that will be all now. Wonderful news. Go and take the rest of the day off. No, take the week off. I'll see you back here Monday morning... oh, and remember to leave the letter with me please.' He smiled but something about the friendly grin made Maria think that it wasn't genuine.

'Thank you so much sir, I'm so pleased for you. I hope you take some rest too and don't worry, I'm sure that whatever you decide you will make the right decision.'

Maria waved as she left the room, closing the office door behind her. The superior leaned back in his chair and lost himself in his thoughts for a few moments. So, the Big Chief was definitely dead.

His network had crumbled; his associates were either dead or arrested awaiting trial. The black spider web that hung over the country had finally been destroyed.

Decades of work were finally completed, yet the old man was not thinking about his victory. Swiping the letter that sat on his desk, he picked his phone up and started dialling the number. The black phone rang as it connected to Sir Michael's phone.

'Hello?'

'Sir Michael?'

'I was wondering when I'd be hearing from you. Sorry I had to write in the end. Bit of a raucous all of a sudden here. I

223

thought you might like it in writing. I didn't expect you to ring my home phone though.'

'I couldn't wait until eight, my friend. I have to know.'

'Sure, how can I help?'

'You found the Big Chief's body, yes?'

'Yes we did, burned alive we think, nasty way to go. Still it's what he deserved.'

'Sir Michael' interrupted the superior. 'I have to know, were there any other bodies near his?'

The other end of the phone was silent.

'Sir Michael?'

'In the area of the manor that the Big Chief's corpse was found…we found no others.'

The superior's eyes light up.

'What, nowhere in the house at all?'

'The only corpse we found in the whole building was one that was identified as the Big Chief. There were no others.'

All of a sudden the colour flooded back into the superior's cheeks. The tone of his voice turned to one of merriment.

'Brilliant news, Sir Michael. Brilliant news. Thanks again, I'll ring you later.'

Before Sir Michael had a chance to think of a retort to his colleague's mood he was cut off by the receiver suddenly hanging up. In the now sun-flooded office the superior jumped up with elation.

The beautiful sunshine that had been previously ignored was now a catalyst for the change of mood. He looked out of the same window he had looked out of previously with melancholic eyes.

The unknown man was still alive. Wherever he was, and wherever he had run to with Rachel, the superior knew he was alive.

The succession to his throne no longer mattered. He knew that whatever happened both would now have a bright future.

As bright as sunshine.

'Come on love aren't you done yet?'

The soft attractive voice came from the bedroom. The unknown man turned away from the body length window in his living room and went to voice that beckoned him.

'Nearly there. I've just got a few more things to do first.' He looked into his love's eyes. The sparkle was back. After escaping the Manor with their lives they had promised to patch up their relationship.

It was he, not her, who had made the decision to play dead. It would take the service days to clear the rubble up anyway so it gave them time to patch up the wounds of the past and talk about starting again fresh.

Originally, Rachel was adamant that she didn't want to settle down with a killer. He had explained to her that he had spent a decade thinking about what he given up, about how his new life had not been worth that sacrifices he had left behind.

She was the only person he could trust and when he found her in the manor, it was as if a lifetime of shackles and pain had suddenly been cast off his body and the spark of life had once again been re-ignited. His decision to give it all up for her and start afresh convinced her that this was the man that she had fallen in love with all those years ago. They were lovers again and they had the freedom to do anything.

'Okay, but do hurry, we have to be at the airport in an hour. Now you are sure that your passport is still valid yes?'

The unknown man smiled, something he hadn't done for years until he met Rachel again. Since then he couldn't stop.

'Of course like I told you, I can use my personal information again, I'm just a normal everyday man again.'

'Not just ordinary,' she said kissing him on the lips.

'My hero... now come on, hurry up!'

'Okay, okay,' he chuckled. He had missed this. The flat was full of life again. After their escape they had found a taxi and taken a thirty mile trip to her house, where she had been kidnapped from just a few days before. This had been their safe haven and where they reinitiated their relationship. Then they had a big idea.

Since the organisation would want him back and his vast earnings from his troubles had barely been touched, the couple was now sitting on a small fortune. When they decided on a destination abroad to start a new life and settle down together, they packed her stuff up, drove back to the flat she had walked out of in the past and were now packing his stuff up before they left.

As Rachel went to the bathroom to freshen herself up, the unknown man went to the drawer next to his sofa. Inside there was a gun, a faded picture of a younger Rachel and an envelope. Until recently, the unknown man would have picked the gun up and ignored the picture but now it was the other way around. He placed the envelope on top and left the gun in the drawer. This would confirm his resignation from the service. He knew that it was inevitable that they would come looking for him here when their corpses were not uncovered in the debris.

'Right, I'm ready. Are you?'

'Yes, it's time,' the couple kissed again. Rachel giggled and hung off her boyfriend's neck, her arms wrapped around in affection.

She noticed him looking deep into her eyes.

The same look that had been replaced with a vengeful stare but had now melted back into its friendlier state.

'What is it?'

'I just…I'm so happy you are back.'

She smiled and kissed him again.

'Come on, time to go.'

'Just one moment. I'll see you in the car.'

'Okay, don't be long!' Rachel opened her handbag and put her big lens sunglasses on. She was going to need them in the brilliant sunshine that awaited them outside.

As she left his view, the unknown man looked around his old home for one final time. He allowed himself a few moments to think of how lucky he had been.

A whole new life. With the girl he loved. He had completed his mission and the Big Chief was dead.

The country was again a safer place. How different his life will now be, how it should have been if he had never taken the job on. Now he had his name back, and identity was his to possess yet again. He smiled and picked his luggage up in the bedroom, then left the flat for the last time.

228

Closing the door behind him he looked outside where he could see Rachel waiting impatiently in the car downstairs. He laughed and dug his free hand into his pocket.

Picking his keys out of his right trouser pocket, he juggled them in his hands. This was the moment he would leave his old life for good. He thought of the death, the terrible things he had seen but then thought of the reward it had brought. The kingpin was dead. That was all that mattered.

He smiled as he posted the front door keys through the letterbox. He picked up his belongings and made his way downstairs towards the new morning.

'No regrets.'

ACKNOWLEGEMENTS

First of all, I would like to give each and every one of you who has bought this book the biggest appreciation I can express. It has always been a dream to write and publish my own work but without the following people I could not have done it.

I would like to thank John Galantini for his fantastic, expansive and moody artwork, which added a whole new dimension to the words on the page. I would also like to thank my friends who read the drafts for this book back when they were just short stories and before the idea of combining the adventures of the unknown man into a novel had even crossed my mind.

Huge thanks also goes to Nicole Ibberson who proofread the early stages when I was looking for an outlet and a massive thank you also goes out to the good people of Amazon, who have given independent authors the chance to publish their work where in the past they would have been turned away.

Last but not least I would like to say a massive thanks to my family, who have supported me and my creative endeavours over the years and my Grandad, who unknowingly planted the seeds of this book in my mind by allowing me to watch James Bond films around his house back when I was a little boy. This book is dedicated to him.

The unknown man will return…